Down a cobbled mews of rare tranquil backstreets, people come to talk, gaze at the garden, have a nice cup of tea and a biscuit, then leave with a small blue bottle of perfume. Captured inside it is scented memory of happy times.

What could be the harm in that?

London is a big city, but paths cross, and get all tangled up. A small misunderstanding leads to a seriously large one.

~~~~~~~

This is the novel that accidentally launched a London perfumery, 4160Tuesdays.

4160Tuesdays Ltd
London W3

The Scent of Possibility

Sarah McCartney

A tale of London people, their problems and their perfumes.

THE SCENT OF POSSIBILITY

Sarah McCartney

Copyright © 2014 by Sarah McCartney

All rights reserved. This book or any bit of it of may not be reproduced or used in any way at all without the express written permission of the publisher except for the brief quotations in a book review or scholarly journal. (If you ask nicely, we might let you.)

First Printing: 2014

ISBN 978-1-326-07657-3

4160Tuesdays Ltd
Proper Perfumes Made in London
ww.4160Tuesdays.com

CHAPTER ONE - DAVID	5
CHAPTER TWO - DAVID	11
CHAPTER THREE - DAVID	17
CHAPTER FOUR - PHOEBE	21
CHAPTER FIVE - PHOEBE	28
CHAPTER SIX – DAVID	33
CHAPTER SEVEN - MARIANNE	40
CHAPTER EIGHT - MARIANNE	46
CHAPTER NINE - CHANDRA	52
CHAPTER TEN – CHANDRA	57
CHAPTER ELEVEN - JESSICA	62
CHAPTER TWELVE - JESSICA	69
CHAPTER THIRTEEN - MARIANNE	75
CHAPTER FOURTEEN - GRACE	82
CHAPTER FIFTEEN - GRACE	89
CHAPTER SIXTEEN - MARIANNE	97
CHAPTER SEVENTEEN - GRACE	100
CHAPTER EIGHTEEN - JESSICA	105
CHAPTER NINETEEN - DAVID	109
CHAPTER TWENTY - JESSICA	112
CHAPTER TWENTY-ONE – GRACE	120
CHAPTER TWENTY-TWO - THE NEWS	123
CHAPTER TWENTY-THREE - JESSICA	125
CHAPTER TWENTY-FOUR - DAVID	129
CHAPTER TWENTY-FIVE - DAVID	135
CHAPTER TWENTY-SIX - THE NEWS	138
CHAPTER TWENTY-SEVEN - C.I.D.	141
CHAPTER TWENTY-EIGHT - JESSICA	146

CHAPTER TWENTY-NINE - C.I.D.	149
CHAPTER THIRTY - JOSIE	153
CHAPTER THIRTY-ONE - HADRIAN	155

CHAPTER ONE - DAVID

Problems Solved

25 Bloomsbury Mews, London WC1

Your appointment is at: 4.45 p.m., 6th October

I read the card again, turned it over to see if there were more clues on the back, but there was nothing. The envelope was marked "Personal" so – unlike the rest of the post – Alice hadn't opened it before she put it on my desk. It was handwritten, with a stamp and a London WC1 postmark.

Had Alice been loitering to see what I did when I opened it? I'd managed to get cappuccino froth on my nose and when she came in with the post I was a little distracted. By the time I'd dealt with the coffee issue, she'd gone back to her desk.

I checked my desk diary where I found that between the hours of four and six there were no calls or meetings arranged. To be fair, it was a Friday, and I did have the occasional gap. Usually Alice or Grace would pencil in those times for admin, but perhaps they were hoping for an early start to the weekend. Next, I looked at the back pages and checked the central London map to calculate how long it would take me to walk there, then wrote in on my recently acquired electronic calendar.

For the rest of the day, between the hours of ten in the morning and four in the afternoon I answered emails, went to meetings and enjoyed a pleasant, although somewhat hurried, lunch with the deputy head of my accounts department. At 4 p.m. a reminder popped up on my screen.

"Go to appointment," it said. And so I did.

Walking swiftly along Theobalds Road, it crossed my mind that I had no idea what I was going to find when I got there, and that my behaviour was rather out of character. Ought I to turn back? What if it turned out to be a joke, a trap, or a misunderstanding? As I continued towards Bloomsbury Mews I decided to keep the appointment, just out of interest. I had planned to arrive five minutes early, which is only polite, and which would have given me time to compose myself. The day was fine, the sun was shining and although the air was autumnal crisp I could keep warm as long as I kept moving briskly along. So I did. As a result I arrived with twenty minutes to spare, so I dropped into a genuine Italian coffee shop just around the corner for a macchiato and a muffin.

Bloomsbury Mews had long ceased to house the carriages, horses and grooms of the Victorian residences behind them. The stable buildings had been converted into homes, and the occasional office building. Had I been single, I should have enjoyed living there, a quiet backwater almost in the centre of town. The ground still had its granite cobbles, which did their best to trip me up.

Number 25 had a big old black door and looked rather subdued compared to the neighbours. There was 23 with its navy blue painted window frames. Inside, halogen lights shone from huge aluminium lamp shades on to desks below. It had a large Perspex block sticking out, hanging perpendicular to the wall like a pub sign. I knew that look. It was either a design agency, or a company that made large Perspex blocks. Number 27 appeared to be a private residence. Its bright red wooden door shouted "visit me!" and dominated the buildings on either side.

Still with four minutes to spare, I paused before ringing the doorbell. I couldn't remember a time in the last two years when I'd walked out of the office without somebody knowing where I was going. For the last 10 years I'd known - more or less - what was going to happen next. Then I rang the doorbell.

An ancient buzzer sounded, there was a heavy click, and the door invited me to push it and walk inside. I was in a long corridor, illuminated by wall lights of a plain, modern design. At the end I could see a black door, with a window at the top, behind which I could see a tree.

"Come down the corridor and turn right," called a pleasant female voice with perhaps a hint of a regional accent. I did exactly as commanded and walked into a small room. It had a low ceiling; that's what I remember most about it. I'm tall, and this room was built for short people, or servants whose comfort was secondary to function. Nevertheless it didn't make me feel uncomfortable, unlike most low ceilings, probably because I could see outside into an absolute treasure of a garden.

"What extraordinary colours," I remember saying, as I saw the reds and golds of autumn leaves in the sunshine. It made me feel happier than I'd been in a while. This worried me slightly as I found myself in completely unfamiliar territory, on an unplanned visit to a previously unknown street in the same room as a woman I had never met before, and happy at the same time. An unusual combination.

"As you're here," she said smiling, "why don't you have a seat?"

I sat on a slightly worn, velvet upholstered armchair which was a good deal more comfortable than it promised.

"So how about telling me exactly how you came to be there this afternoon," she said, sitting down opposite me.

I smiled back; it was partly a response to her friendliness and partly in amusement that she had read my mind. I took out the card, and explained how it had arrived on my desk.

"So here you are," she said, looking at me straight in the eyes from her modern red leather chair slightly to the right of the window. I ought to explain that her smile was like an encouraging, welcoming endorsement of my presence. She wasn't laughing at me, nor was it one of those fake stretches of the mouth that one receives from blank-eyed sales assistants the world over.

"Next," she asked, "How would you feel about describing your day, from the moment you woke up?"

"I don't mind at all," I said, "I assume that if you want to know it must be relevant." She smiled.

I told her everything from the alarm going on, dragging myself from sleep, getting ready for work, trying not to obstruct my wife and daughters, leaving the house, getting a precious seat on the tube, grabbing a nap, picking up my coffee and arriving at the office, opening the post, meetings, emails, lunch and my walk."

"Good," she said. "Thank you."

"If you don't mind my asking," I said, "how on earth did I end up with one of your cards on my desk?"

"Good question." Then she added, "Would you like a cup of tea?"

"I would rather, if we have time," I said. "Medium strength, splash of milk, one sugar."

She got up and walked into the hall, opening the opposite door into a tiny kitchen with a window that let in an equally tiny amount of light and looked out at a yellow brick wall. I stayed in my comfy chair while she boiled the kettle, clinked a couple of cups and took the milk from the fridge. Back she came with the tea which she'd put on to a metal trolley with black rubber wheels, just like the one my grandmother had had. 1930s or 1940s I'd have guessed, what's known these days as shabby chic, I believe.

"You got your card from someone who's been here before, someone who thought I could help you. That person decided you needed this appointment more than she did." She smiled again and I was just about to answer when she added, "It's not as mysterious as it sounds; it's just the way I work, by personal recommendation, anonymous or otherwise."

"I'm not at all certain that I do have a problem that needs solving," I said. "But as I'm here, and I have a cup of tea to drink, perhaps I might ask you what exactly it is that you do." We both tested our tea. She had elegant hands with nails cut short like a piano player's, and I attempted to gauge her age from them. 35 or so, I would say, if I were asked to give evidence. She was wearing black, like the anarchist girls at university, although rather more smart. Hair dark, eyes dark, some shiny stuff on her lips which marked her teacup. She had small wrists and an old gold watch. Her collection of rings seemed to be placed randomly, with no marital significance, but I'd say she had an air of independence.

"What I do is this," she said, "I listen to people's problems. I make recommendations, and it's entirely up to those people whether or not they follow them. If my visitors feel that their problems are solved, they can pass on their next appointment card to someone new. If they think that I haven't helped at all then they are free to come back and tell me all about it, or to disappear forever. So, I'm delighted to see you today because I know that you've come to me from someone who trusts me, albeit in a rather unusual way."

"As I was saying though," I said, "I'm struggling to work out why the person who sent me here thinks I have a problem."

She took a long deep breath and stared intently at the Oriental carpet beneath her feet then after she exhaled, she said,

"Tell me a little about your life." Then looked at me, from my feet slowly all the way up to my eyes, where she fixed me with a steady gaze and smiled again. As I felt myself relaxing into her chair I wondered if she had put something strange in the tea. The room smelt of biscuits.

"I'm the managing director of a small printing company," I said, "which produces items of the most beautiful quality for customers to whom quality is important. I own some shares, but the majority are held by the family who set it up in the late 19th century. Some of our customers have been with us for as long as records go back, and most of them come to us by personal recommendation. There, we have something in common."

I paused to see if that was the sort of thing she wanted to know. She nodded, so I continued.

"I live in Chiswick, in a house I love, which we bought 15 years ago when prices were reasonable. I share it with my wife and our two daughters, who are both attending the local school, a rather good state place, thank goodness. I suppose you might look at my life and consider it to be quite dull. We take a couple of holidays a year, usually in Europe, but this year we went to Northumberland. I do the garden, which gives me a great deal of pleasure, and this year we've been growing our own vegetables. Loads of courgettes and baskets full of runner beans. My secret indulgence is in treating myself to well-made clothes and shoes which I hope no one would notice. I got that from my dad."

As I thought about the way I summed up my life I felt a sadness, something which I'd been avoiding, that weighed me down in the comfortable velvet chair. I looked at my handmade shoes and found that I had nothing more to say.

"May I ask you why you like to sleep every morning on the tube?" she said gently.

"It's because I'm tired," I said, "I sleep on the way home too."

"What is it you do that makes you so tired?" she asked.

I had to think hard about that. I'd read that on average one needs eight and three quarter hours sleep a night but we get about seven. We build up a sleep debt and, given the chance to pay it off, we can sleep up to 14 hours quite comfortably. I supposed that I came in at around about seven hours sleep every night. Midnight to 7 a.m. I go to bed after Marianne has gone to sleep and I get up about the same time as she does.

"I don't think my wife loves me anymore," I heard myself say.

CHAPTER TWO - DAVID

"I'm going to make another cup of tea," said my new confidante. "Then you can explain to me how you got from falling asleep on the tube to believing that your wife no longer loves you."

For the first time she looked serious. She moved like a cat, a mature cat which had outgrown its kittenish clumsiness, as she got up from her chair and strolled across the hall.

"I'm not quite sure where it came from myself," I called through to her. Then I walked across the hall and put my head around the kitchen door. These things can't be shouted.

"The thing is this; I get up early and I go to bed when I'm absolutely certain she's already asleep. I try not to disturb her. It's the look of annoyance that she has, if there might be the slightest possibility that I - how shall I put this? - as if any intimacy towards her is some kind of imposition. I go to bed late so I don't irritate her; I prefer to avoid the possibility of rejection."

"I don't blame you," she said, then the kettle boiled so we paused.

More tea, this time with digestive biscuits. Sitting in the drawing room, we looked at each other, sizing each other up I suppose. I was wondering if she could help me and I felt that she was wondering how she could help me. At least we were both singing off the same hymn sheet, as it were.

"I suppose there's a possibility that my marriage is in danger," I said to myself, but out loud. "I think I've known this for some time, years perhaps, but as nothing seems to happen, nothing actually goes wrong, it seemed like a good idea not to bother mentioning it, just in case.

"But if she really is tired of me, and we're just carrying on, staying together for the sake of the children, as they say, then at some point something rather nasty will happen, all at once, and I could almost pretend to myself that I didn't see it coming. And now I can't. I can see it coming. I'm one of those averagely attractive, averagely well off middle-aged men who are open to distraction by a vivacious 23-year-old. I would look a complete idiot."

11

I actually started to chuckle at the very thought of my own potential midlife crisis and my companion smiled warmly too. It was at this point that I realised we hadn't been introduced.

"I'm ever so sorry," I said, "My name is David, David Cavendish. Am I allowed to know yours?"

"I'm Unity Cassel," she said. At that point my phone rang.

"Excuse me, I can't believe I forgot to turn it off." I stood up and took it from my jacket pocket. It was the office; of course it was. I hadn't told them where I'd gone or if I'd be back. "I shall have to take it, I'm so sorry."

As I explained that I'd gone out to a meeting and couldn't say exactly when I'd be back, I could hear the suspicion in the silence at the other end of the phone, or perhaps I imagined it, but I think I didn't. Perhaps my assistants were about to indulge in some speculation about their boss who had sneaked away in the afternoon for an anonymous assignation. How surprised Alice and Grace would be to find me sitting in an armchair in a small room looking at one of London's secret gardens, drinking tea and eating digestive biscuits with an intriguing woman dressed in black.

They say that every man falls in love with his therapist, if indeed this is what Unity was, and I understand that this is because it's their job is to sit and listen. Naturally, she was reading my mind, something it turned out that she was really rather good at.

"How long is it since you sat down and had a good heart to heart with your wife? What's her name?" she added.

"Her name is Marianne, and she's a wonderful woman, but I think the last time we spoke about ourselves and our future was when we were deciding whether or not to have a second child."

"And that was when?" she asked.

"That would be about 11 years ago," I said. Then I just sat there in my easy chair thinking about where on earth the time had gone. After a while I noticed that Unity was silent too but it was a comfortable silence, and it seemed to me that her presence became very small, as if she'd left the room for a while to allow me to be by myself.

"What do you think you might do about this?" she asked after a minute or two.

"I don't know," I said, although I did. I looked at her and she was raising one eyebrow. "All right, yes I do know, but I'm not entirely certain how I'm going to approach it after all this time."

"This might be the point at which I volunteer my help," she said. "If you're interested."

"Please, by all means, go ahead," I said.

"First," she said, leaning slightly forwards in her chair and placing her hands one on top of the other, on her left knee, "I'd just like to warn you that it's not always the 23-year-olds you need to look out for. In your position, it's the single thirty-somethings who're looking for a stable relationship with a man who has already proved himself capable of marriage and children, and could just about afford to maintain a first family and start a second one. And if you know any of those people, then you might like to consider that it's just possible that they have plans for you of which you are completely unaware."

I'm almost certain that I managed to retain a passive expression, but as Unity had already displayed an uncanny ability to read my mind I suspect that she could see that I was feeling worried. My personal assistants answered this description, and one of them had recently broken up with her fiancé over his sudden lack of ability to "commit" as she put it. I had taken her out to lunch once or twice - perhaps more - to commiserate, and I realised that I might have put myself into a slightly delicate position.

"Yes," I said, "I do see what you mean."

"There is another thing to consider," she said, "that Marianne might be attracted to another man, but is fulfilling her part of the bargain that you made when you agreed to have your second child which is, correct me if I'm wrong, the unspoken acceptance that you will provide for the family and she will care for you all, with the right to return to work when she feels it appropriate, until such time as your children have gone to college, or left home, or gone completely wild. So once you do start to talk about this, it could become more complicated than you imagine."

"Until today," I said, "I hadn't imagined that it was complicated at all."

"That's because you had forgotten how to use your imagination."

"Fair point," I said, and I picked up my tea but realised that my hands had started to shake. She noticed of course.

"There is something I think I can do to help," she said. "I'd like you to speak to Marianne, but it doesn't have to be about anything serious. Please don't go barging in announcing that you have to talk. There are better ways to start a conversation. I'd like you to be kind to her this weekend; just think about that and act on it.

"Right now, I'd like you to think of a place where you've been very happy, when you were a child or when you were growing up or just recently. That doesn't matter; just tell me what it was like. No hurry."

I leaned back and I thought; after a while I realised that my eyes were closed and the picture I saw was my grandfather's shed. It was a grand affair for a shed, right at the end of his garden, more of a bolthole than workplace. It was where he used to read books to me, and store the apples and pears from his trees and smoke his pipe, which would never be allowed these days, not in front of the children.

"Tell me about it," she said, "What did it smell like?" I was surprised, but I told her.

"Wait here," she said, which made me smile as I wasn't intending to move. She left the room and I heard her open a door then go upstairs then she was above me treading on some ancient squeaky floorboards. For a few minutes all I heard were occasional footsteps and then she came back downstairs. She produced two strips of paper and a small blue bottle. Taking the top off, she dipped the papers into a liquid and gave one to me. It smelled of tobacco, fruit, old books and garden sheds. I was close to tears. She had found a lost memory; the house in Sussex where I had spent joyful weekends and endless summer holidays. I smiled with amazement, with wonder.

"How did you do that?" I didn't really expect an answer. She seemed delighted.

"You like it?" she asked, showing much less composure than she had managed to keep so far. I sniffed the paper again, deeply. I wanted to wrap her in my arms and hug her, but I didn't. She handed me the bottle.

"It's for you, but you must use it wisely." She grinned as she said this. "I'm serious though. You can wear this. You can use it to help you feel the happiness you felt in your grandfather's shed. Wear it to give you confidence; use it to help you be kind to Marianne."

"How on earth am I going to explain...?" I asked, not quite able to explain what it was I wanted to explain. "How am I going to describe you? What do you even do for a living? Am I to say that I visited my local white witch, right in the heart of Bloomsbury?"

"Let's think about this," she said, "I could be your business coach, or your personal mentor or something suitably jargon-esque."

"Personal brand consultant!" I said, "That's what people have these days, and it would give me a good reason for smelling of my grandfather's shed, rather than the usual toothpaste." I was getting ready to leave when I remembered something crucial. "I haven't asked your rates, what do you charge; how shall I pay you? Shall I come back? How often? Was I supposed to ask all this at the beginning?"

"We had far more important things to talk about," she said, "but this is the way that I'd like to do things. Please come to see me again this time next week if you can. Each time you visit I shall give you an appointment card but if you meet someone you feel needs it more than you do, please pass it on. Some people come here once; others visit several times. There are some I don't think I'll ever see the back of. I would like you to reward me appropriately, but anonymously, by placing an envelope with a suitable amount through the door one day. It's for you to decide how valuable our meeting has been.

"One last thing," she added as we were walking along the low corridor to the front door, "and that is to point out that people who are, if you don't mind my saying, slightly set in their ways, only start to wear a new scent when something interesting has happened in their lives. Questions might be asked. Your wife could be suspicious; but that might not be such a bad thing, under the circumstances."

"And be kind," she said, as she closed the door behind me.

There was no one else in the mews, so I took out the bottle and dabbed a drop of scent on to my lapel, and then on my wrists too. I breathed in. In the fresh air, it smelled even more wonderful. I could see the lines of garden tools, his leather Chesterfield chair that grandma had banished there when the arms had worn through, and the racks of apples that stayed fresh all winter as long as they were stored perfectly. I felt that my eyes had been opened to a different route, that I was seeing not just what was in front of me, but what was behind and inside me. No, it didn't exactly make sense to me either, but that's the best that I can do. It was all new to me.

There was a challenge waiting. In general, I would spend an hour or so after my official work time, loitering around the office making sure that every last detail was attended to. I'd get home at eight, to bid a passing greeting to my daughters, help with the difficult homework if required, then sit down for a quiet dinner, watch television, pay the bills and go to bed, late. This evening I was ready to go home on time.

I returned to the office where Grace and Alice were waiting. They glanced at each other. Grace was the one who had recently split up with her cad, the man who had decided that she wasn't "the one".

"I'm off now," said Alice, "goodnight David."

"Goodnight Alice," I said. The building was quiet. The directors' offices were empty; they were rarely busy, but we kept them tidy just in case. As it was Friday, the others had left on time too.

"I'll stay to help you finish off, David," Grace said, but I looked around and decided that whatever needed doing didn't need doing before Monday morning.

"No, it's all fine here," I said, "I think I'll go straight home for a change. You can have the evening off too." Did I notice a slight pursing of the lips and a line forming between her eyebrows?

"That's an interesting cologne you're wearing?" she said, smiling and standing a little too close. "What's it called?"

"It's called Grandfather's Shed," I said, "and I got it from my personal branding consultant." Yes, without doubt, there it was; the eyebrow lowering, lines forming and lips pursing. Best nipped in the bud before it takes hold, I said to myself, but I shall remember to be kind. The day before I wouldn't have noticed, but things were different.

CHAPTER THREE - DAVID

Enthused by my extraordinary afternoon, I left the office despite Grace's offers to help, and got home early, earlier than I'd arrived of my own volition at my own front door for years. I gave myself a quick top-up of my reassuring scent, dabbing a little on to my shirt cuffs, and I found myself smiling over slightly foggy memories of the times I'd spent with my grandfather. They were blended with sharper, brighter recent thoughts of the cosy room in Bloomsbury where I'd spent half the afternoon. Breathing in a good lungful of the stuff, I let myself in and found Marianne in her newly, extended, all-mod-cons kitchen-stroke-dining room with a friend of hers I knew vaguely and a man I'd never met. She looked astonished; in fact they all did. Perhaps I did too.

"David, what on earth are you doing here?" Marianne said in a way that suggested I'd broken in through the window or just arrived from China with no advance warning.

"I live here," I said, rather stupidly perhaps, and did my best to smile benignly at the assembled company. They'd opened a bottle of white wine, and as Marianne saw me glance at it; she picked up a glass, composing herself again, and said,

"Well, come and join us," adding, "You know Josie, don't you? And this is her brother, Mack."

Mack and I shook hands. He was a handsome rogue of a fellow, all dark hair and twinkling eyes, perhaps a few years younger than Josie and five years younger than me. An odd situation to find myself in, but as I'd paid for the house and the wine, I was uncommonly determined not to allow myself to feel uncomfortable.

"Poor Mack has just had a break-up with his fiancée," Marianne said, "We were discussing the advantages and disadvantages of being in a committed relationship."

I wasn't certain but she looked, I thought, somewhat cynical as she said this, with her mouth raised at once corner and lowered at the other. My wife was also looking uncharacteristically glamorous for a Friday

17

evening at home. Her friend Josie was not long divorced, if I'd remembered correctly the stories I'd heard about it all. Her ex-husband was living alone in a flat nearby, having confessed to an affair with a colleague and consequently stripped of the family home, car and the like, then promptly deserted by the other woman. I inadvertently sighed with relief at the thought that I still had possession of my front door key and the statutory right of entry to my home.

"Sorry to hear that, Mack," I said reasonably non-committally, I thought, and took a sip.

"Actually," said his sister, "I think it was a lucky escape. She sounded clingy to me. Couldn't wait to leave work and play the housewife! I think Mack ought to play the field a little, have some fun before he settles down." She glanced over in an unpleasantly knowing way towards Marianne, who was staring at her glass and expressing what could be described as a studied attitude of indifference. What had I walked into?

"And how are you, Josie?" I asked, "And the children?"

"Oh, I get by," she said, "And the boys are a delight, as always, filling the house with noise and mud and electronic things. Jessica's a permanent mystery to me, her and her brains."

"Where are our dear children, by the way?" I asked Marianne, grateful to be back on solid ground.

"David! They're away at your parents' for the weekend," she said in the exasperated tone of the unfortunate wife whose husband doesn't listen to a thing she says. "I'd imagined I'd be home alone all evening, until Josie and Mack dropped by."

Was I wrong, or was I not? Was I imagining it after my interesting afternoon and the discovery of my newly awakened consciousness? Was there a little conspiracy here from which I was excluded? I thought perhaps yes, but that it would be wisest to feign ignorance.

"Well, we must be off, my dears," said Josie, considering leaving an elegant few millimetres in her glass then slugging it back after all, and sliding off her stool by the breakfast bar. "Won't keep you!"

Marianne fluttered about and mildly begged her to stay longer, perhaps for dinner? But she went after a great deal of polite social posturing, taking Mack with her. On the way to the door as she passed me and grazed my cheek with an apology for a kiss, she stood back and said, "That's an interesting fragrance you're wearing, David. What's it called?"

"Grandfather's Shed," I announced calmly and didn't volunteer to explain.

"Hmm!" she said, with eyebrows raised at Marianne and a smile in the direction of her younger brother. And they were gone, thank heavens. My wife strolled through to our sitting room and sat down; I followed not far behind.

"So the girls are away until Sunday," I said, sitting, recalling that I had known this, had I given it any thought. "Would you like to go somewhere this weekend?" It had been a while since Marianne had given me such a stare. She raised her eyes slowly from her glass, furrowed her brows and glared at me. I met her interrogatory gaze with what I hope was a warm, but not overly enthusiastic smile. I had already surprised her once today and I didn't want to alarm her into a squabble.

"Do you have plans?" I asked, "Because it's not important, just an idea."

"No, yes," she said, looking back down at her glass. "No, not really. What were you thinking of?"

"I hadn't thought about it at all," I said, "It just occurred to me."

She stared at me again, but with less suspicion, a little more curiosity.

"You mean to say that you're suggesting something spontaneous?" she asked, with a hint of a friendly smile, one I recognised but which had become rare in recent times. What had happened to the pair of us? She had a wonderful smile.

"Is that a yes?" I asked with some humour, I hoped, "Because if it is, perhaps I ought to book something now before I lose my nerve." Marianne smiled, so I walked next door to the computer room and switched on. The scent of autumn fruit, warm wooden walls and pipe tobacco gave me the courage I had hardly realised I'd lost, to do something other than the usual thing.

"Would tomorrow morning be convenient?" I called as I checked availability on the Eurostar.

"Fine," she called back, which was a little disturbing, because even I realised that fine can mean the absolute opposite. Nevertheless I had decided that I had very little to lose and a marriage to regain, so I booked us first class on the ten o'clock to Paris and a rather elegant suite in a quiet hotel just off the Place des Vosges. Of course I realised that this had the potential to intimidate, a pity that the promise of a romantic weekend away could be perceived as a threat. I determined to do whatever it was that Marianne wanted to do and nothing that she didn't, while at the same time doing my level best to ensure that we ate well and relaxed a little. That was my plan.

"I've booked a taxi for eight-thirty. I hope that's not too early for you?" I called. And with that, I had taken one more step in my quest to stay awake on the journey to work each morning.

CHAPTER FOUR - PHOEBE

One of my colleagues, Chandra, from the IT project planning department, caught me snivelling into my hankie in the stationery cupboard. I mean! I hardly knew him. All I'd ever noticed about him was that he smelled really tasty. Does that sound terrible? It does, doesn't it? I mean, he wasn't really my type, so I'd not paid any attention. Too nice! The thing is, a couple of my mates had dated Asian boys and it all ended in disaster. They were great, it was great, it was all fine – until they'd met their mums and dads. There was Angela, Raymonde and Lynette; all three of them had been going out with these lovely boys – kind, generous, although one of them was a bit flash, good looking but actually faithful and attentive – then they'd asked to be introduced to the parents. Oh dear. Not good. There had been these massive rows and tears before bedtime. Mum and dad - and a whole load of aunties - had bailed in and told them to leave their sons alone and go out with nice white boys. Which, frankly was none of their business. I thought. But it made me think twice.

Actually, to be fair Lynette did then meet a nice Asian boy whose parents were cool with it and she got married to him. And also to be fair Angela had not taken Riz home to meet her mum and dad yet either, so I'm not going to judge. Except it was a bit on my mind when I'd seen Chandra before, and given him a good sniff, all cinnamon and lemons and something that smelled like I'd imagined magic carpets would, that there wasn't likely to be a future in it because probably he had a traditional mum and dad who were still hoping that he'd marry a good Asian girl, like an accountant or something, not like me who'd wasted her school years and just ended up being in customer services with not much hope of career development, even though I was hoping one day that I might start training to be a yoga teacher in my spare time. Which is how I knew what Chandra meant in Sanskrit and I said to him,

"Hello Mr. Moon," and I tried to look like I was looking for something useful, like bulldog clips or a ring binder or something instead of running away from that lying, cheating tosser of an international sales manager who had never said he was "engaged" last year when he was doing the verbal communications skills workshop, and staying in that nice hotel right on the river, where he said that I was just what he'd been looking for all his life. And all this when his mates knew all about it, and about me as well. Who, then, cheeky bastard, turned up later for his management skills workshop with a blokey "engagement" ring on his finger and people were shouting congratulations at him because they all knew he was getting married – right in front of me - and I felt a right fool. And today, he's back for a week of meetings with a view to moving into the London office but apparently the engagement is all off, so he thinks it's fine to slide over and said how nice it would be to "renew our acquaintance". Well, I'm not that stupid, but I'm not as tough as I act, so because my cheeks were burning bright red and I felt like I might cry out of shame or humiliation and a bit of disappointment too - yes, I said it, I was disappointed that he turned out such a slime ball and that I couldn't ever trust a man like that - so I was hiding in the stationery cupboard and in walked Chandra. And I said,

"Hello Mr. Moon," like I said I'd said.

"Phoebe," he said, Chandra, that was. "You know my name!"

"You know mine," I said.

"But I don't know what it is in Hindi," he said and I said, "Neither do I," and then neither of us knew what to say next and we were in a very small cupboard and one of us had to leave pretty soon or else people would talk.

He gave me this card, and he said, "Take this," and then he just reversed out, grabbing a pack of recycled A4 paper so it didn't look a bit odd, him leaving the stationery cupboard empty handed. Then I realised that he must have come in there just to see me, and that was nice of him, and then I read the card.

It said:

Problems Solved

25 Bloomsbury Mews, London WC1

Your appointment is at:

Then in neat writing in what looked like proper pen and ink, there was a time and date, for the following week, just after work. So I went there. I thought I was going to be meeting Chandra, but I didn't.

I looked it up on the web and then checked it on my new phone with maps, which is really useful, because I've done that before, looked something up online, and thought I remembered it and then got lost and had to call Raymonde to get her to look it up all over again. It was raining so I put on the trainers I keep in the bottom drawer for just in case. So I looked a right idiot, like those American women in the last century who came over to the City and went to work in tea-coloured tights, Burberry macks and big hair with a pair of bright white Reeboks at the bottom, to make them look like they worked hard and played hard and all that rubbish. Except that these were quite nice grey and black Pumas and they were OK with black tights and besides it was raining so it's allowed.

I got the bus down to as close as it goes, then walked up the road avoiding the white vans that were splashing through the puddles by the kerb. I was wondering what it was that Chandra had planned exactly; maybe it was a support group for people who got themselves into dead-end relationships. We would all sit around and tell each other all about the times we convinced ourselves that his one had a bit of potential, only to find out that he'd been using up a bit of time while his fiancée was flat hunting for both of them. For example.

The street was cobbled and really nice, quiet with no traffic to splash you. It was a good thing I'd not worn heels. Cobbles are quaint but they do screw up your shoes. It looked like the kind of place they'd film a Dickens serial for the BBC on a Sunday evening. I mean, they would show it on a Sunday evening; they would probably film it Monday to Friday. Except they would have to computer graphic out the modern bits, but I didn't suppose that was all that hard. Just cut and paste one of the old bits over the top, maybe.

I hadn't told anyone I was coming, so as I was a bit early, I texted Angela to ask her to call me in two hours' time and - if I didn't answer - to send the police round. It was our standard procedure for blind dates, internet meet-ups and other potentially dangerous situations. Just to be on the safe side. Although there was that one time when the police kicked Lynette's door down because she'd had such a great night out with this man she took him home then forgot that that she'd forgotten to set the alarm and hadn't turned up at work. He'd got a bit of a surprise too, although he did agree to see her again. But just the once.

Number 25. It was a black door, really old looking and solid and with a big knocker so I knocked it, then noticed there was a normal doorbell too, but I'd got so carried away with the Dickens thing I thought I was Estella or Little Nell or someone and forgot to look. As I was deciding what to do, the door buzzed me in anyway, so I pushed it and went inside. The funny thing was that I felt as if I knew the place, déjà vu, but I could swear that I'd never been there before. It smelled of cake shops, which made my mouth water a bit, because I'd not eaten since lunchtime and that was just a sandwich.

"Come down to the end and turn left," said a bright, singsong woman's voice. I'd been expecting a big hallway and an imposing staircase, but instead it was a long corridor, down a couple of steps, along some ancient slabs of stone, all worn down at the middle. It was bright though, with nice lighting that gave it a good atmosphere and shone up at the wonky ceiling that matched the wonky floor. It was a bit of an adventure.

Her head popped out from a doorway along at the end. Dark hair, tied in a way that I've never worked out how, so that it looked a bit arty but stayed up despite itself. Dark eyes, eyeliner, bright lipstick; she looked like one of those creative women who run galleries or make massive abstract tapestries for the foyers in buildings like the one we work in. I followed her into her room. What a place! It was like something from a magazine, just smaller. It had two antique chairs upholstered in bright, modern fabrics and a couple of reclining chairs that looked either like art deco like she'd got them yesterday from IKEA. Difficult to tell sometimes. Through the blinds I could see the rain dripping off fading autumn leaves on to a stone paved bit and a little lawn.

"Is that your garden?" I asked. I would really have liked a garden but I lived in an upstairs flat with my friends. On nice days we went to the park, but it's difficult to sunbathe when you've got lads kicking footballs at you, the winos wandering over with the 15th can of extra strength lager wanting to chat you up, or the middle classes letting their kids throw stuff at you and telling the annoying little monkeys how clever they are.

"Yes, it is, "she said, "I'm lucky."

"It's funny you say that," I said, "Because most people just complain about what they have and forget to count their blessings. Have you noticed? Most people would say, 'yes and it's a real nuisance because I've got to rake up all those leaves this evening,' and you're supposed to sympathise with them when really you want to say, 'you lucky lucky people!' "

"Yes," she said, and she smiled at me. "Coffee?" she said, "I can do a good caffe latte."

"That would be just right," I said.

She popped off next door to get the drinks done, and when she came back she'd brought home baked biscuits too. This woman was unreal! We sat down and talked about the rain for a bit.

"Is Chandra going to be here too?" I said. "He's my friend. At least, he's not exactly my friend, just someone I know, but he seems like a good kind of a lad and he gave me this card so I thought, 'Why not?' and here I am." And I thought I would wait to see what she had to say because I still wasn't sure what it was that we were planning to do. She crossed her legs and I noticed she was wearing a nice pair of black flats that I'd seen a couple of weeks back in Selfridges. Not cheap either. Then again, not flashy and you wouldn't know they were expensive, unless you happened to know, which is my idea of quite well dressed. I'd like some of them when I was a bit older. Talking of which, I'd have guessed maybe 42, 43?

"Ah, no he's not coming over today," she said, "He sent you here to see me. I'll explain, but first, I'd be interested to know what the circumstances were which led to your arrival in that chair." she said, "In other words, how come he gave you the card?"

"Oh dear, that's a bit of a story!" I said and settled down to tell it. "The short version is that I was in tears in the stationery cupboard and he came in and gave it to me. Leading up to that, well, this man turned up at the office. I'd met him before. He's sort of a bit older and a bit sophisticated and very good looking in that dark, Celtic, smouldery way." I laughed a bit thinking about how that sounded.

"He was at last year's annual training week and I'd thought that he really liked me and he was staying in London, and I was a bit drunk but not totally, so I knew what I was doing... And naturally I thought that this was the beginning of a relationship and he was really nice about how soon he'd see me and how I ought to go over and stay with him in Ireland, which is where he's based. Then after that I overheard this man saying to his friend, 'Did you hear that Cormac pulled again? He's a terror! And he's engaged to that posh girl isn't he?' And you know how it is when you feel your insides all freezing up, but you still keep smiling and pretend you don't care and it hasn't really happened. I wondered if maybe he'd made a mistake, but no, next time he turned up with the ring on. So, fine, I'd been a bit stupid. I stopped returning his emails and his texts and I got on with getting over it, which wasn't that hard since he wasn't in town. Then he turned up again in the office and said how nice it would be to "renew our acquaintance" and I said that I thought not and I smiled and walked away, but it was totally embarrassing and I felt like rubbish and I know I was going all red and I did not want to give him the privilege of seeing me all messed up so I waited until he'd gone and walked straight into the stationery cupboard. Then in came Chandra."

"And he gave you his appointment. That's the way it sometimes works here."

"Oh right," I said, although I didn't really see how it worked, "That was nice of him, though."

"Yes it was," she said, "He's a very nice man, although that's all I shall say about him because of course I don't talk about the other people who come here." We both smiled and I wondered how well she knew him, exactly. What else was there to know?

"So what made you decide to come along?" she asked me.

"Well...," I said, "What's your name?"

"Unity," she said and I must have looked a bit confused because she said, "Yes, my parents actually named me that. Unity - oneness."

"Oh right," I said. It wasn't such a bad name, just a bit unusual.

"So," she said, "What was it that brought you here? Do you have a problem that needs solving?

"I do, Unity," I said, "Because it was just at that moment Chandra gave me the card that I'd been thinking to myself that I had completely screwed up my life. I'm stuck here with no degree and no prospects and no bloke – although that's a separate subject entirely - and I was just thinking that I looked like a real idiot and in he walked. Yes, I've wasted my life and I don't know what to do about it. That's about it! Solve that one!"

CHAPTER FIVE - PHOEBE

I took a biscuit from the plate she offered me and crunched. Tasty. Unity just nodded and looked as if she was having a good think. Then she sipped her coffee and asked me,

"What would you have preferred to do with your life, if you'd done it differently?"

To be honest, I'd not got around to thinking about that; I'd only just realised that I'd got it all wrong. So I took another bite of the oat biscuit and said hmm to myself.

"Did you make these?" I asked her while I gave it a bit more thought.

"Yes, I did" she said. "I like to do a bit of baking when I get a moment."

"I've never baked anything, don't know how," I said, "Another thing I've not done!"

"Now don't start feeling too sorry for yourself," she said, but not in a nasty way, "I could teach you to bake if you like; it's not hard and it impresses people quite out of proportion to the skills you need to do it." She held out the fancy but ancient china plate and I took another one. "What else haven't you done that you wish you had?"

"I messed up at school," I said. "It's quite simple. I was one of a bunch of girls who decided not to do anything much. We didn't bother with homework, we didn't join the band or do gym or swimming or anything that won us badges to sew on our blazers. We decided that everyone who did that stuff was very uncool. Then when it came to results time, it turns out that for most of them that had just been a cover story; once they got home they would do their homework, their mums and dads took them to private oboe classes or whatever, they did really well, applied to universities, all disappeared off and left the three of us who'd bought into it all stuck at home wondering what had hit us. I'm easily led, aren't I?"

"If you know you're easily led, then you're one step closer to being able to make up your own mind," she said. "But I'm interested to know what your mother and father did differently from the other girls' parents. Didn't they make you do your homework?"

"Oh no," I said. "I think they were just happy to think I'd be staying at home with them instead of going off to Newcastle, or Bristol or miles away. They never went to university and they were quite relaxed about whatever I wanted to do. As long as I didn't go really bad, that is, which I didn't. Just got a bit drunk at parties sometimes and yelled at them when they said I should put more clothes on to go out. I live just down the road from them now, in a flat with two other girls."

"How old are you?" she said, "If you don't mind my asking."

"Twenty-six," I said miserably because I was closer to thirty than twenty and it was all going to start going wrong. Then I looked at Unity and saw she was smiling at me, like a friendly aunt, as if she was going to pat me on the head and say, "Aw bless!"

"It's old!" I said. "No offence."

"None taken," she said and thank the lord she was still smiling because some people get really offended if you mention age.

"So are you saying that you wish you'd worked harder and gone to university?" she asked me.

"I think what I'm saying is that I wish I hadn't been so - what's its name? – gullible sometimes, like following cool girls around school and getting fooled by good looking blokes."

"Is there someone whose life you admire, someone who you think has got it mostly right, that you would like to emulate if you could?"

"Emulate? What like copy?" I said, "Because I've spent too long copying other people."

"Not exactly copy, but live your life in the same kind of way, but with your own style, in your own direction."

I was thinking about that, and then Freda Fletcher came to mind. She was four years above me in school, always unbelievably sophisticated, elegant and wonderful in every way, considering she was from Walthamstow too. I used to tell myself that I'd be like Freda when I was older, and ask myself what Freda would do. Then of course, I'd go and do something different and a bit stupid. I was in awe of her, I suppose. So I told Unity about that.

"What's Freda up to now?" she asked me and do you know what? I had no idea.

"It's been five years since I heard anything about her," I said.

"What do you imagine Freda's up to right now?" she asked, sitting up and looking right at me, before she took a sip of tea and smiled at the cup.

"I don't know," I said, because I had no idea.

"Do me a favour and use your imagination," she said. "Given what you know about Freda, what she was like at school, how do you think she grew up? What would you hope had happened to her?"

"What? Guess, you mean?" I asked her because I wasn't sure if I was allowed to make it up.

"Absolutely!" she said, leaning forward with her hands on her knees, encouraging me as if I was trying to learn to ride a bike or ice skate or something.

"I think," I said, "..." and my mind went blank.

"Hang on a moment," said Unity and she dashed out of the room. When she came back the room smelled like she'd opened the door into a greenhouse full of herbs and flowers. She must have been off to water the plants, although I did think that they could have waited another 10 minutes, probably.

"Right," she said, "You were just going to tell me what you think Freda might be doing now."

"Yes," I said, "She went on to college and although she had planned to study geography, she discovered geology and travelled the world collecting rocks and photographing mountains. That sort of thing?"

"Absolutely," said Unity, "Then what?"

"She met a handsome geologist and they went off into the desert in Africa and they nearly got completely lost, but they survived because they were determined to live, and they discovered a new rock, well not new, because it was really old, obviously because it was rock, but new to them and he named it Fletcherite after her." I just kept going and

Unity kept saying, "Then what?" until I'd come out with a whole life story for Freda, who'd taken a jewellery course and learned how to set her Fletcherite rocks in sterling silver settings, married the geologist, settled down in Leeds and had three children, was still amazingly beautiful, happy and contented.

By the time I'd finished I started to laugh, and Unity joined in and when we'd finished I said to her, "But I still don't know what I want to do, do I? I've still screwed up!"

"But your imaginary Freda didn't know either, did she?" said Unity. "She just kept finding things that interested her and followed the trail." We were both speaking quite noisily, then Unity sat back in her chair and quietened down a bit, and so did I, although I was still thinking about Freda, and myself and my life back at the office.

"What shall I do?" I asked her.

"I'll make a suggestion," she said. All I want you to do between now and your next appointment is to notice interesting things you'd like to follow up. Not the things you've missed out on or things you tell yourself you can't do, but things you could do, might possibly do in future. Write them down if you like."

"That's not too hard," I said.

"No it's not, but it's harder than you might think, so I have some things to help you."

She produced a small notebook with a golden cover, a pen and a small blue bottle. "Smell this," she said, took the lid off and handed it to me. It was the herb and flower greenhouse scent I'd noticed earlier. I just looked at her amazed.

"You can put that in a bottle?" I said.

"Better than that," she said, "You can wear it. You can scent your special notebook with it. You can use it to remind yourself of your task."

I felt a bit embarrassed all of a sudden and I mumbled a bit, "I'm not sure I can afford to pay you that much," and as we stood up she put her hand on my arm and said, "Phoebe," which was odd because I was almost certain that I hadn't told her my name.

"Phoebe," she said, "Don't worry about that yet. You can pay me when you can, if you can. And don't forget the deal. If you see someone who needs to come here and talk more than you do, pass on the card – but don't go giving it away on a whim! Ask yourself, "What would Freda do?" and if you think Freda would keep it for herself, then come back."

I dabbed a little of the greenhouse scent on to my wrists and took a good sniff. It made me smile. It made me think of Freda.

"Was it a real greenhouse I could smell, or was it this?" I asked her.

"It was this and a bit of your imagination," she said, "Use it."

As we walked back down the long hallway, she said, "I very much hope to see you again," and I thought to myself how much I would really like to come back.

It had stopped raining but everything was wet still, and it was dark, streetlights shining in the puddles. The granite cobbles were slippery so I watched my step and made my way back to the busy streets where buses and bicycles reminded me I was in the 21st Century. I passed a small pub that I hadn't noticed on my way down here and looked in. There he was, the two-timing, handsome pain in the backside, with a bunch of my colleagues. There also, in the bunch of colleagues, was Chandra. As this was one of those pubs which had just had its carpet taken up, its curtains taken down and its lighting lowered, they could see right out at me, which they did.

His face, a look of certain triumph, a knowledge that I would walk in there, unable to resist his charms for a second time. I breathed in the smell of greenhouse flowers and opened the door.

"Chandra," I said, walking up to my new friend, "Do you fancy going somewhere else for a beer or two?"

CHAPTER SIX – DAVID

So we went to Paris. Marianne seemed pleased but astonished at the whole idea. We set off early, got the train, had a champagne brunch, did a spot of shopping and stayed in for dinner at the hotel's own restaurant. It had a star so it seemed silly to trek somewhere else in the cold. I knew that Marianne would expect me to make a move, as it were. So I decided not to drop even the slightest hint, to be nothing more than an interested, good friend of hers. I could have been one of her chums from the gym, off on an adventure, no strings attached. We had a splendid meal, drank an excellent red wine and strolled back to our delightful room, arm in arm.

There are times when I feel that Marianne walks around the place naked, or in her underwear, just to irritate me, because she knows that she has absolutely no intention of following it through. She has the power to make me want her, and she abuses it. The result of this, I feel, would eventually be that I simply stopped caring. I had got too close to that point. In Paris, I was determined not to hand her the power.

So for that night I switched off. I had decided to be celibate. I refused to be disappointed by hoping for something which was in her gift, which she could choose whether to bestow on me or not. So, although I didn't ignore her, I decided to play the role of her best gay friend, and the astonishing thing was that she decided to convert me, so to speak. Instead of being an imposition I had become a challenge, and so, entirely at the instigation of my wife, and reciprocated by me, we took a step back towards the balance of power being equal.

On the Sunday we strolled around le Marais and over to the Ile de la Cité before turning up at the Gare du Nord to take the train home. We talked rather a lot, about many things. It felt unfamiliar, pleasantly so, like a new start.

That Friday, I pondered, then decided to keep my second appointment with Unity. I'd considered handing my card to Grace. She seemed to be struggling to reconcile herself with her newly unbetrothed status and I felt sorry for her. However, after I had perhaps allowed her to assume a closeness to me that I did not reciprocate, I wanted to re-establish our boundaries.

So no, Grace did not get the benefit of a comfortable couple of hours with Unity; I kept them for myself. I also took an amount of cash from my bank account and placed it inside a card I bought at the British Museum shop. I took into account the cost of a bottle of cologne, a couple of hours with a top consultant and added a small sum towards the opportunity cost of a failed marriage. I hoped that she would not be embarrassed by the amount, but in my experience people rarely turn down generous donations. They might protest, but then they find a way to justify to themselves that they deserve it.

Her little sitting room smelled of roses; I looked around for the flowers, then smiled as I realised it was probably another of her potions. I could never see the point of roses with no scent. I had planted several in the back garden, one in the front too, and become fond of the scented ones. The decorative ones, visually impressive but lacking in fragrance, seem to me to be heartless objects, like beautiful women who feel that their looks are sufficient contribution to a social gathering and never offer to split the cost of a cab.

I was wearing a drop of two of my precious liquid. It blended well with roses, I thought. Grandfather's shed had had a clambering old rose growing up one side and over the roof. It occurred to me that this might be why I was so fond of them. I was opening my mind to associations and observations; some were pleasant and some were not. Finding a strange, single man in my house, drinking wine with my wife, was one of the unpleasant ones, particularly as he had the self-satisfied air of one who is confident around women. Nevertheless, as far as I was aware, he had not made a return visit. I had decided to tell Unity all about this and ask for her views.

We sat down with our coffee and I was preparing to relate the interesting developments in my life since I had last sat in her green chair.

"I'd like to know more about Marianne," she said, before I had composed myself and decided where to start. "Where did you meet?"

"It was at my aunt's 60th birthday party," I said, recalling Marianne in her shiny golden dress and high heels. "Her mother was my aunt's friend. We were both practically bludgeoned into coming along by our respective parents to lower the average age. We had the opportunity to talk and found that we liked some of the same things, you know. I think we were reading the same book and we'd just watched the same film. It rather seemed like fate at the time. Of course I forgot to take her number, but then my aunt called me and gave it to me, then chased me for a fortnight until I called her."

"Why didn't you call her straight away?" Unity asked me.

"Do you know how it feels when you're looking forward to something, but that this something could possibly go wrong?" I said. "For example, I have a friend who tells me he is restoring an old Jaguar. At some point he must take it for an M.O.T. so he can drive it on the road, but he never does. If it isn't finished, then it can't fail its test. It was rather like that. I could say to my friends, 'I've met this girl,' and describe her and imply that we might go out soon. If I called her and she turned me down, then it was all over and I'd have to start again. It was almost better not to arrange a first date – just in case it turned out to be the only one."

"So you called her and you lived happily ever after," said Unity, smiling.

"You could say that," I said. It seemed odd to be talking to Unity about Marianne. Almost a betrayal of our private secrets. I would have felt almost the same way telling Marianne about Unity.

"Would you explain to me, if I'm not treading on sacred ground," she said, reading my mind once more, "what it is about Marianne that makes you want to be with her."

"Marianne and I...," I started to say but came to a halt. "We... whatever I say will sound clichéd, I suspect," I said. "However, I admire her. She is fair and honest. She has supported me and always accepted the way that I do things. I'm not the most adventurous of people, but she hasn't complained. Her friends perhaps have more exciting lives, and the most excitement we've had recently was knocking down walls and putting in RSJs for the new kitchen and conservatory. Then if I really think about what I like about our life, it's that she makes it all rather beautiful."

"Beauty is important," she said.

I agreed.

"And Marianne herself, is she beautiful?" Unity asked.

"I do believe that she is," I said. Of course I think she is, but I also think that others agree with me. I took out the photograph I carry of Marianne and the girls and showed it to Unity. I took it at a crèperie by the beach in Brittany. They with their naturally light hair, she with her carefully highlighted colour, wearing bright beach clothes, looking relaxed and cheerful. Unity smiled as she looked at it, and handed it back to me.

"Indeed she is," she said. "And your aunt and her friend had decided that you were ideal for each other, which is always a good sign," she said.

"We went to Paris the day after I came here," I said, wishing to update our conversation to the present.

"That sounds like a definite move in the right direction," she said, leaning slightly forwards in an encouraging way, so I decided to tell her more. Then I remembered the evening before we left.

"There's another situation on which I'd appreciate your opinion," I said, and she raised her eyebrows, nodding, to give me permission to continue. "When I got home early, for the first time in months, her friend was there - a nice enough woman, divorced recently and a little unpredictable – and she'd brought her younger brother over. The thing is, that although there's no real reason why she ought not to take her brother anywhere she wishes, I wasn't certain why exactly she'd taken him to our house. I felt as though I'd arrived on the wrong day at someone's tea party. Then they left, rather awkwardly I thought, although I'm probably wrong. Then I booked the trip to Paris."

"Mmm. Yes, you were probably right," she said. "It's rare to pick up the wrong signals in a situation such as that, although it's very easily done by email. Never trust your instincts with emails, by the way. But when you're in the same room, that's different."

"So would it be unreasonable of me to suspect that this woman was introducing her brother to my wife with some ulterior motive?" I asked.

"Not unreasonable, but as it appears that no harm was done, it's probably best to ignore it and concentrate on yourself. Keep an eye open though," she said thoughtfully. "Would you like to tell me a little more about Paris?" she asked, and given the reason I'd come to number 25 in the first place - and that a trip to Paris would probably be an improvement in our relationship - I thought that it was a fair request.

"Well, as they say in the corporate training sessions," I said, "the elephant in the room is that I told you I thought my wife no longer loved me. I now believe that there is a remote possibility that we have the chance to rebuild something of our marriage. Perhaps something better. Of course, only last week I had managed not to notice that it might have fallen apart, and now I think that by some extraordinarily fortunate intervention I've spotted it just in time.

"So as I was saying, I got home on Friday to be introduced to this chap, and I decided not to comment on his unexpected appearance, and just to treat that as if it were absolutely normal, the sort of thing that happens at my house between the hours of six and eight, because to be perfectly honest I have no idea what usually happens. I suppose I imagined it would be something like the happy families on TV ads, the girls getting home from school and doing a bit of homework, playing on the computer, telephoning their friends and chatting about boys while Marianne made dinner."

"Maybe that is what they do most of the time," she said.

"I rather hope to find out by being present more often," I said. "I'd like to remind myself of the reasons Marianne interested me in the first place. Now I say this without expecting you to comment or to reassure me in any way, but I believe that Marianne had begun to find me rather dull. I put bread on the table and petrol in the BMW, the rings on her fingers and bells on her toes and all that, and when a marriage descends to being nothing but a financial arrangement, there's space for others to fulfil emotional demands. Do you think that's a fair assessment?"

"I think that was a very good analysis of such a situation," said Unity. "Do you think you're right?"

"I think I was very close to it indeed, and that I had carelessly allowed it to happen."

My coffee had gone cold and I had only drunk a third of it; I glanced at it and Unity followed my gaze.

"You've arrived at a very interesting place," she said, "and I'd like you to tell me more, but first I'm going to get you a new cup of coffee. These things are important."

I could hear her bustling about, clinking cups in the kitchen across the way, and I paused to consider exactly how much I was going to say. By the time she got back I'd decided that I might as well change the habit of a lifetime and tell her absolutely everything.

I picked up my coffee, and took a test slurp. Too hot.

"I don't feel quite comfortable telling you this," I said, "but I'm determined to do my best." Unity nodded, and looked serious, gentle but nevertheless fascinated. I don't know how she does it. So I told her.

"I want us to have a fair, balanced marriage again, some kind of equality. I don't want all the control; that's not my way at all. And I would like equality of giving rather than equality of taking away. I'm not at all certain that I making any sense, but it's helping me to get my thoughts in order so I'd appreciate it if you would bear with me."

"Yes, you're most definitely making sense," said Unity, so I continued.

"And I also believe that if I did take away her power, by not caring at all, then she would find someone else to beguile. Perhaps that someone was going to be her friend's younger brother, at least for the time being. And by changing the way I behave, ever so slightly, by coming home early, going to Paris and, not ignoring her exactly, but certainly appearing a little less needful, I seem to have rekindled her interest. As it were. Do you follow, without my having to spell it all out?"

"I do," said Unity. "And why do you think she changed her view?"

"I believe she finally considered that she might be in danger of losing me, and that she wasn't entirely happy at the thought."

"Well, you are behaving remarkably oddly," she said smiling, "compared with the last few years."

"For a start," I said, "I smell like pipe tobacco, fruit bushes and Chesterfield chairs."

"And women notice such things," said Unity, "because such a small change in behaviour normally indicates a huge change in attitude."

"It's a strange thing about that magic potion you gave me though." I said, "Everyone comments upon it. I've named it Grandfather's Shed and I've told them you found it for me, but I rather implied that it's part of my new personal brand identity."

"But that is exactly what it is," said Unity, "if you choose to see it like that."

"That makes me feel a lot better," I said. "I don't like to feel that I'm deliberately misleading people. But there is something about scent isn't there?"

"There most certainly is," she said smiling at me, crossing her legs and leaning back into her sofa.

CHAPTER SEVEN - MARIANNE

I found the card in my husband's jacket pocket. I copied out the details and put it back. Yes, of course I knew it was wrong, the last refuge of the suspicious wife, and I hated myself for doing it, but I did it and it's done. I wanted to take a look at the person who'd changed my husband's perspective on life. To be perfectly honest I was angry. But if you'd asked me to explain I wouldn't have been able to tell you exactly why. I had thought – I'd been certain – that I was completely in charge of our marriage, and then it seemed that I was not.

David had been 100% boringly predictable for nigh on ten years and at the point at which I'd decided that I was free to behave exactly as I pleased, he changed. You could set your clock by him, as my grandmother used to say of my grandfather. When he got home two hours early, I actually thought that the clock was wrong!

I used to joke with my friend Josie that if he had an affair, I probably wouldn't notice. Honestly, he was so little trouble, I'd have let him get on with it. He was almost invisible, but he did pay the bills. Josie, of course, had had a much more volatile marriage, and when John had strayed with his available younger colleague, she felt deeply betrayed, which was what turned her so vengeful. That, of course, and guilt about her dalliance with the man along the street who walked his dog in the park every morning.

It was as if she'd punished her husband for the sin of being caught, breaking into bits and confessing, rather than for his unfaithfulness. To be honest, I think she'll have him back when he's been sufficiently punished. In the meantime she's living her life vicariously through Mack, setting him and his unfeasibly good looks loose on unstable relationships everywhere.

And I almost fell for it, didn't I?

Then everything changed. I found myself packing an overnight back for a chilly, cosy weekend in Paris. I actually enjoyed myself; it was as though I was spending time with an ex I'd split up with years ago and we were checking out the territory to see if there was any possibility of picking up where we had left off.

But I still didn't know where I stood. I asked myself if I really felt nothing at all for my husband. If he left, would I care? And I had to acknowledge that although I'd managed to neglect them, hide and starve those feelings of nourishment, they were still there. They were alive and could help or hurt me. All the same, I simply could not explain why he had suddenly changed in this way, unless it was the obvious, the cliché, paying me extra attention to assuage his guilt at the embarrassingly age-old answer, the Other Woman.

But that didn't seem right; he seemed to be paying me and the girls, more attention, getting home early, talking to us. When would he even have the time to see someone else, unless it was lunchtimes? And the Paris trip. How was I to explain that? It was wonderful. But why?

Personal Brand Consultant. That is how he described her. The appointment card was ambiguous. Of course I oughtn't to have looked in his pockets, but desperate measures were called for. Problems Solved, it said. Do personal brand consultants solve problems? Was this an elaborate cover for meeting his new mistress? Is mistress even a word that people use this century?

Nothing about him seemed to have changed but his attitude and his strange new habit of wearing a fragrance, one which was completely different from the lime cologne he usually bought from his barber's shop. We know why men start to wear fragrance: the same reason women buy new underwear. Someone new is taking an interest.

The card told me he had an appointment for late Friday afternoon. How long would it last? An hour, 90 minutes? These people charge you for an hour, give you 50 minutes then leave ten for a tea break before the next clients, don't they? That was always assuming that she really was what he told me she was.

None of it made sense to me, but when I thought about it, I found that I lost my appetite and couldn't concentrate on even the smallest task. I'd spent a lovely weekend in Paris with an attractive man, but I wasn't certain if it was a one-off, the start of something new or the end of a marriage that had long since packed its bags and turned off the lights. How strange. Good or bad, I needed an answer.

I decided to go there just to see what kind of an establishment it was. A smart, modern office building with a clutch of lucrative consultants perhaps, or an old established surgery, a converted Victorian town house built in grey stone with small brass plaques by the door. Or worse, an unmarked high class brothel. Perhaps there were two of them, a brand consultant and a mistress. What had happened to my erstwhile notoriously dull husband?

The girls started to take advantage of me while I was so utterly distracted. At one point I realised I'd promised them both new party shoes and bags while I wasn't listening to their questions; they thought this absolutely hilarious – and they were right – and insisted that we go out late night shopping. On a whim I called David and he came straight from work to meet us for pizza on the high street. We enjoyed it, I think. It was just so unusual.

On the Friday afternoon, I secured a safe haven for the girls after school and went into town. It wasn't an area I was familiar with so I finally worked out how to use the satnav on my phone walked from the nearest tube following the instructions. It seemed like miles - new journeys always do - and although it was blowy there was a warm breeze for autumn and the sun glowed through the white sky.

It felt like one of the Famous Five adventures I'd read when I was a child, and I'd always fancied my chances as a private detective, not in real life of course, just a little fantasy. I was excruciatingly nervous though; by the time I'd made it to the final corner I could scarcely swallow. Also I could barely walk as I'd put on my usual black stretch boots with heels. A cobbled street hadn't figured in my plans, but one manages! And there I was at 25 Bloomsbury Mews.

Nor had I imagined that the place would be completely deserted. I'd pictured a city street with a coffee bar every few paces. I would place myself in the window with a cup of tea, a book and a hat, to observe the comings and goings of number 25. Silly of me; when was a mews ever a buzzing thoroughfare? I hadn't really thought this through.

I made my way back to the corner, and walked to the nearest cafe, an older Italian joint, not one of the new chains, with a scattering of individuals eating cakes, drinking their hot beverages and all reading newspapers. It looked like a minor convention of private investigators. So I sat down with my coffee, gazed at my book but failed to notice the words, and wondered what to do next. The man in charge of the place let me nurse my latte for a good twenty minutes after I'd drained the last drop, then smiled at me as I paid, as if he knew exactly what I was up to. Which was more than I did.

Taking a moment to pause, I wondered what on earth I thought I was doing. A reasonably attractive, reasonably contented mother of two with a kind, generous husband - who had recently started to confuse me - venturing into central London to indulge in an afternoon of light espionage.

I timed my departure for exactly 90 minutes from the start of David's appointment and strolled back to Bloomsbury Mews, paused at the corner and peered into the street in a manner that anyone watching would think suspicious.

My timing was terrible, or perfect, depending on your point of view. David was just coming out of number 25, although I couldn't see who was at the door. As he walked towards me, he was looking down at the cobbles so I managed to scuttle with very little dignity back the way I came, into the deepest doorway I could find, hoping that no one would want to come out or go in until David had disappeared. There was a 50:50 chance that he would walk right past me and stare me in the face. Then how silly would I look?

I quickly decided to claim this place as my osteopath's surgery and pretend that I was just leaving if he caught me, or turn it round and demand to know what he was doing out of the office. But he didn't. I left it for 30 seconds – I counted – and walked out with my head held high, by which time he was already 50 yards in the opposite direction.

Determined not to back out I walked right up to 25, taking care not to break an ankle negotiating the cobbles, and rang the bell. When the door opened, I was surprised to find a tall man behind it. He was dark, West Indian roots, I would guess, with a mass of long dreadlocks, very good looking, mid thirties perhaps. I would trust him to advise me on my personal brand issues, but I wasn't certain that I wanted to have him solve my problems.

"Hello," he said, "Can I help you?"

He was neither friendly nor cold, but he did seem surprised to see me.

"I was just wondering what it was you do here," I said a little tentatively. "A friend of mine has been talking about you and I was thinking perhaps you might be able to fit me in, at some point...." and I tailed off as he just looked at me and waited for me to finish.

"We don't normally work exactly like that," he said, "But why don't you come in and we can talk about it." I followed him along a corridor which was surprisingly rustic for Bloomsbury, positively rural. The floor was uneven, paved with stone, so I still had to watch where I placed my heels. The wallpaper was interesting though, just on one section of the right hand wall, with brightly coloured humming birds, vines and roses. Not horticulturally correct, but very beautiful.

"Are you OK?" asked the man, because I'd stopped to admire the wallpaper and he'd just realised that he'd lost me.

"Fine," I said and walked after him, clattering a little along the flagstones. Through a window at the end of the hall, I could see fading sunlight shining on tree branches at the back. I wondered what the building was that we were walking under, who owned the upstairs houses, how did this little place come to be built at all?

"Mind yourself," he said as we turned right at the end and climbed up a narrow staircase, with a thick silk rope to hold on to and a worn striped carpet up the centre. Two steps squeaked loudly, the other 15 squeaked softly and upstairs opened up into an airy room that looked like an artist's studio. Architecturally that is. There were no paints, easels or canvases strewn around the place, but it did have a high, north facing window at one end.

Along the centre was an immense table. Goodness knows how it ever got up the stairs. Perhaps it was built there from slabs of pine; it looked a hundred years old at least. The rest of the furniture was an eclectic mixture, from bright 1950s with Formica surfaces and primary coloured handles, detouring by way of the arts and crafts movement and returning to the present day represented by a modular office in one corner.

Sitting at the desk was a small, white woman with untidily tied up dark hair.

"Thanks, Carl," she said, and she swivelled the chair round, stood up and came over to me. "Welcome to number twenty-five. How can we help you?"

"I'm not sure, to be honest," I said, "But you came highly recommended." I'd hoped I was getting away with it, but I was bluffing horribly and my face was beginning to warm up and glow. She put her hands together and lifted them up towards her face, in the way that yoga teachers say thank you at the end of the class, and I had no idea what she was going to say next.

"Shall we have a coffee?" she said and she smiled at me in a way I might describe as knowingly, if that didn't sound ridiculous. But she did give the impression that she could see straight through my pretence. Or perhaps it was just me, worried that my subterfuge was showing.

"That would be wonderful," I said, knowing that if I had another coffee so shortly after the one I'd had around the corner I would be likely to babble irresponsibly and confess everything, my amateur sleuth impersonation, shadowing my own husband and wanting to get inside this place just to find out exactly what she'd done to him.

"We'll go downstairs," she said so I just followed her. I was beginning to regret all of this. Stairs, silk rope to hang on to, squeaks, corridor, left turn into a small, cosy sitting room that smelled of roses. I sat in a huge dark green velvet wing chair that reminded me of my auntie's front room. It was that exact moment at which I started to feel less agitated. The wonderful Carl came in with two frothy coffees, smiled, left the room and closed the door. My companion now had me cornered, but she slipped off her shoes, folded her black-trousered legs beneath her and curled up, cat-like, into her stripy chair opposite me, and leaned back, holding her coffee cup in both hands. She watched the door close then slowly turned to look me right in the eyes, then she smiled, gently.

"Let's start again," she said, "Because I think you'll feel a lot better if you tell me the whole truth about how you came be standing on my doorstep."

CHAPTER EIGHT - MARIANNE

"Oh my God, this is so embarrassing. You can see right through me can't you?" I said, mortified. "Is it quite obvious that I'm lying my head off?"

"Not at all," she said, smiling with a twinkle in her eye that looked as if she was almost going to start to giggle, "It's just that around half an hour ago your husband showed me a photograph of you with your two daughters looking extraordinarily happy on a holiday in Brittany."

"I do feel so incredibly stupid," I said, "Would you like me to leave? I could just go now so I don't dig myself into this any deeper than I already have." I put my cup down and picked up my bag.

"No, please don't do that," she said, "You've gone to all that trouble to get yourself here so you might as well find the answers to your questions."

I began to see why it was that David came here, because despite my feeling so ridiculously childish, I also felt welcome and I actually felt no desire to pick up my things and go. But what was I going to ask her? You don't actually come right out and accuse someone of being your husband's mistress, do you? Actually, perhaps you do.

"Why don't I start?" she said, "My name is Unity Cassel, and I help people to solve their problems. I can't tell you exactly what it is that David and I talk about, although I imagine that once you've got to know me slightly better, you'll have a rough idea. I can definitely tell you though, that I am not in any kind of relationship with your husband apart from this one, but I am the person who supplied him with his new scent. Does that explain a few things to you?"

"Oh lord, Unity," I said. "That pretty much explains absolutely everything." I was so relieved that I just started crying but I didn't really know why. It had been a very odd week.

Unity gave me a handkerchief, a proper one made out of white cotton with tatting around the edges of the way my grandmother used to make them, and waited for me to be able to speak again. I had a few goes, gave up and then realised that there wasn't much hurry.

"Marianne," Unity said, "you found the place, so I'm thinking that you found my appointment card."

"I did." I said.

"And you saw that what I do is to solve people's problems," she said, "so I suspect that somewhere deep down you might have one of your own that you'd like to talk through with me. Because, after all, you didn't have to ring the doorbell. You could have found another way to do a bit of sleuthing."

I think I probably blushed a little at that.

"I don't quite know what I was thinking to be honest," I said, "I imagined myself as one of Enid Blyton's adventurers I think, just without the dog or the other three. I'd got myself rather confused, even before David came home smelling of his grandfather's tool shed or whatever it is you gave him, and after that my life just turned upside down. I mean to say, it's not that bad is it? Some people lose their homes, or are getting shot at, or don't have enough to drink or eat and I'm sitting here worrying that my husband smells different and has started to come home on time. For goodness sake, I don't know I'm born! I don't really have any problems do I? And, what's more, I've started to babble because this is my second cup of coffee in an hour."

"And I can't deal with the kind of problems that people have when they lose their homes, and are getting shot at or are starving," said Unity, "so we're probably just about equal."

"Your chap, Carl," I said. "He said to me that you don't normally do things quite like this. So I was just wondering how you normally do things. Am I allowed to ask how David found you?"

"I can tell you how everybody finds me," said Unity, "And it's because they're given one of my cards, either by me, or by someone else. No one has ever turned up without a card before, but I'd like to congratulate you on your ingenuity and not scold you for breaking the rules. People come to see me, we talk, they change things a little, and when they decide that they can do it by themselves then they pass on their next appointment card to someone they think needs me more than they do. I'm like a pair of stabilisers for a child learning to ride a bike."

"And the scent?" I asked.

"Do you like the smell you noticed when you walked into this room?" she asked me.

"I absolutely love it to bits," I said. "It's like walking along a garden path and strolling into a fragrant cloud, then having to walk back and find exactly where it came from and smell it more deeply so you can drink it all in."

"I'm glad," she said, "because I feel the same way about that one. And I think that you're a woman who does appreciate the beauty of the things you notice in this world, and values those things, when you stop to think about it."

"I don't know how much David has told you about me," I said, "and I know that I can't ask you, and I perhaps I ought to feel a little more uncomfortable that this, but for some reason I don't. Although I am getting a little bit jittery, but that's most definitely from all this coffee."

"I won't be a moment," said Unity and she left the room. I heard the clatter of plates and back she came with a pile of flapjacks, soft squidgy ones with currents in. "Nourishment," she said, "to take away the jitters. Made them myself." So we sat there and ate biscuits. Of all the things that I had visualised happening at 25 Bloomsbury Mews, this hadn't been on the list.

"So now you're here, and while we're sitting comfortably," said Unity, "why don't you tell me what you plan to do the rest of your life?"

"The rest of my life?" I said, "I haven't got as far as wondering what to make for supper yet."

"I find it helps to have a plan," said Unity, "even if you change it once in a while. But if you don't have a plan you can't check to see how well you're getting along with it."

"Do you know what?" I said, "I think I was just hoping that someone else would do all planning for me, and all I would have to do is argue about it a bit. I suppose that would mean that if it all went wrong it wouldn't be my responsibility."

"Had you given this some thought?" she said, "Or did it just occur to you?"

"I've been thinking about this since we got on the train to Paris last week," I said. "David asked me almost the same question, but I suppose you know that." She shook her head so I continued.

"Yes, he asked me if I'd considered what life would be like when the girls have gone to college, or got married or decided to move to Denmark or whatever it is that they end up doing, because you can't control that can you? And when David retires we're just with each other. Honestly, I suppose it seems odd that I hadn't thought that far ahead into the future but he told me this story. It seems that when he was small he used to go to stay with some cousins who lived in Madrid.

"His aunt worked very hard, did all the cooking, had a part time job teaching cookery in an high school college, looked after the household and his three cousins, and was really the kindest and most generous person you could imagine. His uncle would come in from work, say hello then plug his headphones into the television and watch the news. He joined the family for meals but then just seemed to complain about life in general, or make jokes. His aunt used to chide her husband for drinking too much or eating too much but they seemed to get on perfectly well.

"Then one day, his uncle just left. For the previous few years he'd been carrying on one of those Southern European affairs that apparently everybody knew about except the auntie. Except that he actually left and went to live with his mistress.

"The family kept in touch with their aunt, who busied herself by being a grandmother but as far as everyone knew she never had another relationship. She had this dignified, righteous air of someone whose life has been ruined by sadness, none of it her own fault.

"Then one day, out of the blue, his uncle turned up on the family's doorstep, in England, with his new wife. What was remarkable about her was that she was the absolute spitting image of the original auntie, but the difference was that she adored him. It was only when David saw what a marvellous relationship the two of them had that he realised how bad the old one had been.

"When he poured himself a glass of wine, his new wife would join him, rather than criticising his drinking. When he got home, his new wife would welcome him, rather than asking why he was late and wailing

49

about the meal being ruined. No one mentioned the likeness, but while she was out of the room, his uncle started to talk about his new wife.

"He told David's family that as he'd approached retirement, he'd asked himself what was his life going to be like with her 24 hours a day, and decided that it was going to be intolerable. He simply could not face the constant criticism, the reluctance to accept him for who he was and what he did and he decided that he'd rather be alone. He moved away from the area, and was delighted to find someone who loved him for himself. Not the mistress, incidentally. She'd been married too and stayed with her husband.

"Thinking over it, David saw his uncle's previous marriage in a different light; as a child he'd just seen it as the way it was, as life as normal at his uncle's and aunt's house; they bickered, so did a lot of people. But once he reached his 20s, when he was beginning to look around for someone to be with forever, he deliberately looked for someone who accepted him, like auntie number two rather than auntie number one. David chose me because he wanted to be able to retire and spend 24 hours a day with me. That's how far he planned ahead. And that's why he asked me how I felt."

"What a wonderful story," Unity said. "Is it true?" And I told her yes it was, and that I had met his uncle and both aunties, and that while auntie number one was kind and generous to us she complained about how difficult it was to be kind and generous all the time, her conversation was punctuated with sighs and regrets for the way her life had worked out, with slight digs at everyone around her, but that's the way she'd always behaved, even while she was married. Auntie number two was always smiling, and commenting on the things that she and her husband had in common. They were so happy, they were an inspiration.

"I need to ask you something," I said to Unity, as we paused to consider. "Do you think I can take my husband at his word?"

"You're here under exceptional circumstances," she said, "so I think I'll bend my own rules. Yes, as far as I can tell, with the benefit of my experience, I don't think he has any reason at all not to be truthful with you. What are you going to tell him?"

"Oh my God," I said, "Shall I tell him we've met? I suppose I'll have to, you know? If we're actually going to do this thing, make plans for... for forever. It's best to be open and honest, isn't it? Can I do it, do you think? What on earth will he say?"

"I think, if you do it for the right reasons," she said, "You could turn this into as good a story for your children as the story you just told me."

"I'm going to have to wait for the coffee to wear off," I said, laughing in a slightly panicky way, "and perhaps help myself to a couple of G&Ts."

"But perhaps not," she said, "Stay here for a moment, won't you?" She unfurled herself from her sofa and lightly left the room in her expensive Italian flats. I heard her walk up the stairs, 15 quiet squeaks and two loud ones. She came back with a small blue bottle and gave it to me.

"Wear this, and it'll help," she said, so I dabbed a little on my left wrist and sniffed. It was the scent of the roses in the room. Or rather the scent of the room; there weren't any roses.

"It's remarkable," I said, "Is it for me? She smiled and nodded. We talked about the way roses mean so many different things, and it only as I was about to leave that I remembered to ask, "What do I owe you?"

Unity told me about the way she worked, and kindly gave me a card for another visit. I put it in my purse, where I'm absolutely certain that David would never dream of looking.

CHAPTER NINE - CHANDRA

I don't know what I'd have done without Unity. It wasn't anything that I couldn't have done myself, really, if I'd put my mind to it. But I didn't know how to put my mind to it. I just didn't have the practise, you know? My mum and dad, like a lot of parents who've done quite well for themselves by working hard and following the rules, wanted to me follow their plans. There was no room for initiative in our household, unless it was to take the initiative to tidy our rooms or do the washing up.

So I did an IT degree. As I kid I used to like fiddling about with computers and my dad had heard predictions that this was where the future would be, so he was keen. Once it was quite clear that I wasn't going to Cambridge to be a maths professor of course; that would have been his first choice.

I'll start at the very beginning. The context is important. Well, it is to me. I was born in London; my brother and sisters were born in Pune which my parents still insist on spelling Poonah because that was the way it was printed on the ancient map of India they brought with them and put on the wall. By the time I got to school I was fluent (as fluent as a four year old can be) in Hindi and English and I had a good old London accent from playing with the neighbours' kids.

At first my dad worked at the Post Office in Fulham and our family lived in a small flat belonging to the friend of a relative. My parents saved to buy their own small house and rented a room to another relative's friend, then bought a bigger house and rented out more rooms. By the time I was born, we had the house to ourselves and my dad owned the one next door. He was <u>still</u> working at the sorting office, putting the hours in, predicting when to rent or when to sell like some kind of magical economic barometer.

My sisters are married to two nice enough guys. They were both good looking when they were in their early twenties. The husbands I mean. I have no idea if my sisters were good looking; they're my sisters. How can you tell? Now they're reasonably happily married couples, with the usual things going on. One of them runs a dry cleaners and the other has a coffee shop that he staffs with cool Brazilian kids and runs from the office out the back. Two kids each, very British, and my mum keeps nagging them to produce more, but they're not going to. She thinks they're still 25.

They were arranged marriages, but this isn't what most British people think. My friends think it's some kind of mediaeval torture, getting married to someone that your parents have picked out for you. But they just work like the algorithms in online dating websites. As long as your parents do a good job and input all the right data, then a successful marriage often occurs as a result.

You get to choose; you don't have to leap into wedlock with the first one your aunties send over. And besides, these guys were already living in Britain; one was the only Asian guy at his whole year at college in Durham, and the other was from Cardiff, which was strange because he spoke English with a Welsh accent not that far away from my parent's Indian one.

My brother is the oldest; his wife came from India from a good family. She turned up with the whole pierced nose and sari thing going for her; the neighbours were a bit freaked at that, and my parents were taken aback at her unchallengeable belief that her opinions were a great deal more important than everyone else's. Still she's a kindly soul, bosses my brother about all the time, but he can take it. My dad treated them as equals – in the spirit of embracing Western culture – so every time one of them got married he remortgaged the house next door and gave them a down-payment on one of their own.

You know what's expected of me, don't you? Three successful arranged marriages blossomed from our household and my parents are dropping hints like bombs. They think I'm getting too old to be attractive. They don't mean that I'm ugly, just that people might start to suggest that I'm not the marrying kind, as they used to say, and my marriageability rating will plummet.

To be honest, a couple of my aunties have come right out with it, prodded me in the stomach with a polished hennaed fingernail and asked me right out, "What's wrong with you, Chandra? Are you a gay-boy? Why aren't you married?" Funnily enough I was teased at school when they thought my name was Sandra. One of the teachers said primly, "We'll call you Sam," and that was that. For fourteen years I was Sam. It was only at university that I decided to call myself Chandra again. Even my parents sometimes call me Sam.

I'm not gay though, although my cousin Rajiv is and this is all part of the story; he's happily married to his second cousin Pari, who's a lovely woman from Nottingham. They share a house in Richmond with a Scottish couple, Ray and Amanda. It's just that Ray and Rajiv are together and so are Amanda and Pari; they rearrange the furniture when the family visits.

They share one Indian and one Scottish kid each and everyone's quietly happy. Wouldn't they rather be open and honest about it? Frankly, no way. I think it's Amanda's dad they're most scared of. They're not sure if he'd be more angry about her being with a woman or a non-European. It's all very nice the way it is, thank you, until everyone opens their minds… in another life maybe.

Back to me though. I visited Unity one day when I'd had a good old chinwag with Ray and Rajiv. You can imagine. They've had some issues of their own to sort out along the way. It was actually quite painful for them to get married to someone they didn't love, and then see their own loved ones marry someone different. Even though it was just a big sham, there's something so serious and beautiful about a wedding, getting all the family together and making promises. They looked as if they almost believed it.

It was strange and poignant for those of us who knew the score. Ray gave me Unity's card and I went for my first visit six months ago. They were kind to me, and did not belittle my relatively small difficulties.

The pressure was piling on; my family was arranging a trip to India. Several young ladies had been flown over to Fulham at great expense. When they had heard that my father's house was worth over a million pounds, they were expecting to see a palace not a three story terraced house, and they had gone home disappointed.

I don't mean disappointed that they weren't going to marry me – that would be presuming a lot – but definitely that they'd wasted a lot of time and were going to have to explain themselves to their own ICA (interrogation committee of aunties) on their return. I met them and we talked and some of them were very nice to look at. I could almost imagine myself married to them, but then I found myself wondering what on earth would we talk about? Perhaps most married couples don't talk much after a while, but I'd like to think that we could start off discussing all our likes and dislikes and find out what we had in common: films, books, music cricket? We had nothing of that. My parents no longer had the algorithm installed. It needed an upgrade and they lacked the processing power.

So I thought about it a lot and eventually I did decide to go to my appointment at number 25. I don't know what I was expecting but this wasn't it. We just talked and talked and Unity managed to get out of me all kinds of things that I hadn't managed to put my finger on by myself. It was no wonder that my parents thought I was gay; I'd never been seen in public with a girl, not by them anyway.

I had more in common with British girls, not any specific colour, just girls who'd been brought up in London. Indian girls were under the same pressure as I was; even being in the same room, we would both feel the shadows of our families watching over our shoulders. The nice white girls I worked with were so far off my family's radar that I dismissed my chances without even contemplating a date with someone I liked.

Then suddenly there was someone I really liked. So then I was stumped. I wanted to find where I belonged, and that's what I explained.

"So does everyone," said Unity, smiling gently.

"I thought it was just me," I said.

"Oh no," she said, "I can state quite honestly, and without giving away anyone's secrets, that at one stage or another, we all feel left out, unless there is something very seriously wrong with us. Do you know the story about the Beatles?"

Which she then told me. We talked about me being the youngest of the family, and how I'm putting off what is expected of me but how I don't want to distress anyone by upsetting the apple cart and doing something rebellious.

"Your parents want you to be happy," Unity said and for the first time I listened to what that really means. When my mother says, "I just want you to be happy," she does it with a sort of desperate wail in her voice that sends me straight out of the front door.

"What do you think would happen if I took home a girl who is not Hindu?" I asked.

"Is she nice?" Unity asked.

"She's marvellous," I said and Unity smiled at my sudden and obvious enthusiasm, "At least I think she is, because she fills the place with cheerfulness, but we've not spoken often and I don't like to get carried away thinking about it in case she turns me down."

"Hmm," was all she said for a while. "What parents fear most of all is that their kids will bring home someone who will make them miserable. If your mum and dad react badly, it's for that reason. They'll blame it on background, behaviour, religion or whatever they spot first, whatever sticks out. But if they're kind, loving parents they'll want you to be happy. You might just have to weather a few storms."

At this point, I was wondering what Unity's experience was of such situations, then there was a light knock on the door and a man as tall as the ancient doorframe put his head into the room and asked if we'd like a cup of tea. We'd been there over an hour. Then when I saw this handsome man, with his dark face and dreadlocks that appeared to have been dipped in indigo, I thought perhaps that Unity might have been through some of the same trials as I was facing myself.

CHAPTER TEN - CHANDRA

Over tea I told her about Phoebe. About how she lights up the room each time she walks in. How her attitude seemed different from the other girls, how happy-go-lucky she was, as if she'd been brought up simply not to care what others thought or expected, but had a smile and a kind thought for everyone.

About how she was seduced and dropped by the company's best known charmer and all round cad who turned out to be engaged already to someone with a flat in Chelsea and a promising inheritance. And about how I was just trying to be around and about and helpful when her team's IT misbehaved, occasionally making her a cup of tea when I was in the kitchen at the same time and hoping that she might notice I existed.

"There is always a possibility that Phoebe isn't ready for this," Unity said but not unkindly, "And you should prepare yourself for that."

"I'm not only prepared for that," I countered, "I am prepared to go for the rest of my life never actually speaking to her apart from on a professional basis. I do not want to embark upon an endeavour that would be disastrous for all concerned." Unity was smiling. Perhaps I was exaggerating a little.

"Let's see if we can think of a way to reduce the odds of disaster occurring, shall we?" she said.

Actually what we did was a flow chart, showing the options. That's my chosen way of dealing with problems. I found that I was in a trap. I felt that I could not approach Phoebe as long as I thought that my parents would disapprove of my marrying a non-Hindu. On the other hand, I couldn't ask my parents' permission, because I was afraid they would say it was out of the question.

I had to admit, once Unity had pointed this out to me, that I would have to do one or the other, and that unless I had a chance with Phoebe, there would be no point in starting a potential argument with mum and dad. So that was it. (At this point I added in a critical path analysis.) I would speak to Phoebe. One day, very soon. Quite definitely. Then Unity told me that she would give me something to help me stay calm, and disappeared out of her traditionally English cottage style room. I was expecting some kind of herbal remedy, a bit like one of Auntie Swati's ayurvedic remedies, but not scent. She gave me a little bottle of scent!

I hadn't been a wearer of fragrance in the past, but this didn't resemble those things that the men in management wear in any way at all. Oddly enough it reminded me more of one of Auntie Swati's ayurvedic remedies. It was spicy with a touch of fresh fruits, a little like mango chutney slowing cooking on a wood fire. I'm not doing it justice. But since that day I wore it, and I slowly got into the habit of saying hello to Phoebe more often.

Unity and I met up every fortnight give or take a week here and there. I enjoyed talking to her although I'm certain she wished I would hurry up and get on with it. The thing is this: if you haven't asked someone out on a date, then you haven't been turned down, have you? As long as there's a hope of success, then there's something to look forward to.

I wasn't quite ready to go ahead and open my mouth to ask the relevant question. A couple of times I'd almost got there but it only came out as, "Cup of tea?" Each time I kicked myself, but each time she said, "Yes please," and gave me her smile, then I could imagine that this was exactly what she would say when I did finally ask her out.

At home, I would turn the conversation to my cousin Trisha who had married a white London man - not particularly religious but officially Church of England - and how well that was turning out. My parents would merely say that her poor family were having such a difficult time explaining it to the relatives and change the subject.

Perhaps they thought that if they just dropped a lot of hints, I wouldn't ever raise the topic directly. It could all be just a theoretical nightmare for them, nothing to do with a real person in a real relationship. So not too much progress in that department.

Then one day, when I found Phoebe looking upset after that dreadful man had been bothering her again, I discovered that she knew my name, and she knew what it meant in English. This was a total crisis point. Mack was in the office, ready to pounce again. Even I could see that he is an attractive type to women. She was in a state of emotional uncertainty; that was all too obvious. I was in a dilemma, but then everything became clear. I would give her the opportunity to see Unity too. That was the very least I could do under the circumstances. I gave her my next appointment.

I waited a week, just carrying on as normal. I knew exactly when she was going to see Unity; it was like waiting for your exam results; you want them to turn up, but you're not sure they're going to be that great and the closer you get the less you want to eat breakfast. Fortunately, I found myself working on an intensive new project which involved many hours around a large table being briefed by the Norwegians we'd just begun to work with.

Unfortunately, I often found myself sitting opposite the sales team, including that awful man. I'd heard a rumour too, that he was first in line to take over the big Scandinavian project. Our MD drifted in and out to see how it was all going, so it must have been quite important. As usual, my department had to make it all work, linking up secure back-up systems and making sure that all the data went to all the right homes on deadline day.

I found that my role was actually quite important, and it was interesting to see that I found myself in some fairly direct disagreements with sales. I was not afraid of them; I knew my stuff. So on the final day, when we had finished the whole project plan, I suggested that we go to the pub, and I knew exactly the pub to take them to.

The rest, as they say, was history.

There are some people I know who met and stuck together like glue from day one. In fact two of them are the parents of a friend of mine; they met in the 1960s at a party, went home together and just hung on in there as happy as you can expect to be. I have cited them in my case against arranged marriage occasionally.

Of course, they did have a lot in common already. This was not a random meeting between two complete strangers from opposite ends of the globe. They were from the same social group, same age, same educational standards; it was almost as if the ethereal aunties of fate had arranged for them to be in the same room one Saturday night in Soho. I wanted to stick like glue to Phoebe. Sticky but not clingy. That was potentially a difficult balance, but it did not manifest itself that way. In fact, it went so well that I could hardly believe my luck.

Then one day my dad said to me, after glancing at mother over the dinner table, "Chandra. Are you 'seeing someone' as I believe it is called these days?"

Honestly I thought I was going to faint. My head went light and my feet went heavy and he must have seen my panic, because he added, "Please Chandra, don't worry, don't alarm yourself, it's just a little question." He attempted a light-hearted laugh. By then of course he knew the answer. Over to mum for the next bit.

"Chandra, we would like very much to meet... your friend," she said, smiling yet looking concerned at the same time, like the time I told her I was taking a temporary job as a park-keeper during the university vacation.

"Well, she'd like to meet you too," I said, confirming that my new love interest was indeed a woman and watching them shed one layer of worry.

"What's her name?" asked my mum, venturing into territory which would as surely reveal the answer she needed as if she had come right out and said, "Is she Indian?"

"Her name is Phoebe," I said, "and she is very lovely. She is 26 and she works at my office. We have been going out for almost three weeks now."

"Fee Bee," said my father gravely. "And what kind of a name is that?"

"I do believe, that it is a classical name from Ancient Greece," I said, hoping to impress or distract him from the issue."

"Ah," he said but couldn't quite bring himself to take it to its conclusion. "So perhaps she would like to come to Sunday lunch, isn't it? And your mother shall make a good dinner for all the family."

"Everyone?" I said quietly, picturing the entire lot of us: brother, sisters, spouses, children.

"Let's get it all over at once!" my mother blurted out, and I realised that they'd all been plotting this. We sat there, eyebrows raised high, wondering who was going to speak next. I just took myself a deep breath and said,

"That would be great, mum, dad. That's a really good idea." And all of us sat back with relief and none of us could look at each other because I think we all had tears in our eyes. Over thirty years of worrying about this moment, and it was done.

Then all we had to do was get through lunch.

CHAPTER ELEVEN - JESSICA

I got my first appointment card on the bus to school. Some random woman just handed me an envelope and said, "This is for you," which was a bit unusual but she was getting off then so I just said, "thanks" and put it in my bag for later.

I didn't want to open it, because the other girls on the bus might have wanted to know what it was and I didn't want to show it to them, not right there and then, because they'd probably just grab it off me and throw it around the bus and say things about it. I was standing near the door and no-one noticed because they were all chatting about homework they hadn't done and boys and what they were going to do at the weekend.

So after another long day at school, during which time I was called teacher's pet (although I don't think the teachers like me, they just don't know what to do with me when I'm polite so they're polite back again) and nerd (even though I don't really know that much more about computers than anyone else but I do wear glasses so that probably counts) and creep (which I don't like much at all, because I don't try to creep up to anyone, but I don't seem to be able to do that "ner" thing that they all say to each other, or be rude in a way that makes people laugh).

The thing is that I do kind of enjoy being nice to people, but it doesn't seem to work on people my age, just old people. So when I get on the bus I say "hello" to the driver and he always smiles and says "hello" back again and that cheers me up until I see the other girls on the bus with their legs all stretched out across the aisle and their hair done up in a kind of sloppy pony-tail French way that looks really messy but sort of just right at the same time and I say, "hello" to them all and they all say, "Hi Jessica," in a drawly bored voice so I don't sit with them because they haven't given me permission, so I stand up by the door.

And that's where I got the envelope. I put it in the inside inside pocket of the backpack so if one of the cool girls starts to look through it to see what I've got, she might miss it because she can't be bothered to look as if she's making an effort. Usually they just tip it up and empty it on to the floor to see if I've got anything interesting, and if it's in the inside inside pocket that people don't know is there because it's fixed with Velcro and mesh with a zip, then it's safe.

If they ever do find it, I'll have to get another bag because it's where I sometimes keep the postcard from Ed, the boy I met on holiday in Scotland, and if they ever saw that I would die. I would. I would have a heart attack and die of shame because they would never, ever shut up about it.

Then when I got home, I opened it and I found the card with an appointment for that Saturday, and some money for the tube fare for me and my mum, or whoever I wanted to take with me, and a guide to how to get into London and a map all printed out nicely and a set of instructions for what to look out for and how to ring the doorbell and such. And it was like a magical adventure for me and I nearly died of happiness because it was like I was nearly bursting with the idea of it.

And although I maybe should have told my parents what I was really doing, I told my dad I was going out with a friend and I would see him later, and I told my mum I was doing the same thing and I'd see her on Sunday night. When I said I was going into town, I suppose they thought I meant Ealing, not actually all the way into London, but if they had asked I would have told them, and it's not as though I hadn't done it before although not actually on my own, but only because it had never worked out like that, not because I was too young or anything.

So I took the instructions and a bottle of water and made myself a cheese sandwich and I put on a bright woolly dress that my Auntie Claire's mum's friend had knitted that I really liked, but I wasn't sure if it was all that, because I know what the other girls would have said if they'd seen it.

I wore my second best but not quite bad enough for school shoes, the leggings I'd got my mum to buy me, and my coat and hat and scarf and gloves and I put everything into my other bag, not the school one, and I set off to the bus stop, which was along the road around the corner.

Then I got the tube and it was the same as when I went with my parents, or with Nicola, who actually IS my friend, but she's at a different school, then I thought I could have asked her to come with me but it was too late by then. I had my phone, which I only use in emergencies because it's a cheapo one because you know how when your parents get divorced and everyone says that each one will try to buy you better things to impress you into loving them more than the other one?

Well they don't. They just argue about who has to buy it and then the one who loses gets the cheapest one possible. Which is why my phone was something like £9.99 and doesn't have any apps at all! Except for making calls and sending texts, so I hide it except if I can't totally avoid it.

So I'd normally not looked out of the tube train window before because I'd been talking to people, but this time I did and I saw loads of things like a graveyard in the middle of an industrial estate! And there was a cow on top of a building (I mean like a cow statue, not actually a really one that had climbed up there and got stuck) and I saw the BBC just before we went underground.

Then it got crowded and I gave up my seat for an old Chinese lady who looked really happy to be off her feet because her shoes were too small. Then it got not crowded again and I was still on with two stops to go, then I got off and followed the map and the instructions, then I realised I was an hour and a half early.

I found this cafe which was really friendly, and the nice man did me a hot milk with caramel in it; he was Italian and he'd come to London ages ago but he still had a really strong accent. He taught me a few words and I found out that a latte isn't a coffee, it's milk, but when Londoners ask for a latte, if you give them milk without any coffee in it they get really cross.

In Italy you ask for a caffe latte, he said, but in London they think it's sophisticated to cut it short. So he asked me what I was doing in town and I decided I could trust him so I told him and he said "Aha!" in a sort of mysterious way and said, "then you are in for a very interesting afternoon, young lady" and normally I don't like being called young lady but he meant it nicely so it was OK.

I asked him if he knew them, and he said yes he did, because they buy their beans at his coffee shop and come in for pastries and sandwiches and they were very nice people and he'd known them for quite a few years so that reassured me quite a lot because when I stopped to think about it, it could be anything at all, couldn't it?

And by the time we'd finished it was time for me to go so I promised to call in again one day and I retraced my steps back to the street with the cobbles, that wasn't called a street, it was called a mews but I didn't know why. And there weren't any cats or anything.

When I rang the bell the door opened and I could see that there were some steps down inside and then a lady opened the door wide and stood back to let me in and said, "Hello, welcome to number twenty-five."

"Hello, I'm Jessica," I said. "This is exciting, isn't it?"

"Yes, it is," she said. "I'm Unity. Come on, let's get started," and she led me down the hall into a really nice room that smelled a bit like sweets, which was excellent. She let me choose my own chair so I went for the one that looked really modern, even though I thought it would be uncomfortable, because it so was cool, but then it turned out to be comfortable as well.

"What did you say your name was again?" I asked because I hadn't really been concentrating, and it sounded a bit like Ooty and I didn't think that could be right, but you never know, do you, in this day and age? She spelled it out for me and then I realised what she'd said, like unit with a y on the end, although I'd never met anyone called that before.

"So what do we do?" I asked her and she said that we could just talk a bit about life in general, but mine in particular and she said she was glad I'd come because someone had left a present for me.

"For me?" I said, "But no-one knew I was coming?"

"You know the woman who gave you the card?" Unity asked and I said, "No, I don't really know her. I just met her on the bus." Then I wasn't sure if Unity was laughing at me a bit and I think I went a bit red.

"I'm sorry," she said, "I didn't explain that very well. I meant that I know the woman on the bus, and that I was just asking if you remembered her."

"I see. Well, I do and I don't," I said, "because I'm not certain I'd ever seen her before so I was thinking that it was a completely random thing that she did, and it was just my lucky day. Like in books. Sort of a fairy godmother? And maybe she wasn't even real, just magic? And I wasn't even sure that this place would be here at all, except that she gave me really excellent instructions."

"She'd seen you before, on the bus," Unity said, "And she thought that you might like to come here. She hoped you would, and she left me something for you, for just in case it all worked out." She reached behind her chair and got out a backpack, one with masses of features, and gave it to me.

It was blue, but dark with a shine on it that just reflected the light in all shimmery and purple when the sun shone on it.

"That's for me?" I said. "It's mint." She handed it over and it weighed a ton.

"Open it, she said."

So I did and inside there were some brown tights that went with my school uniform but these were really interesting with patterns on them. Maybe she'd noticed that mine had some holes in them sometimes, or that I'd sewed up the ladders a bit badly, or that some days I didn't have any even though it was a bit cold, because we were only allowed brown and they were a bit difficult to get your hands on. And there were four packets! And they were all different!!

And then there was a pair of shoes!!! They were flat, black ones like we all wear except these ones looked as if they wouldn't wear out as fast as the ones we get, the ones with the soft soles. We get cheap ones because our mums say we'll only grow out of them, just we don't grow out of them quite as fast as they get holes in the bottom usually.

Actually, it's quite cool to have holes in your shoes in summer, but in winter mine still have holes in them and that's not cool, it's freezing. They were the right size too, which was good because I think possibly my feet might have stopped growing for now because I've been the same size for about a year, so maybe they'll last me a bit longer than usual.

And then there were these school things that made me think that I'd got to be asleep and dreaming. There was a massive set of 20 Hi-Tec C pens with 0.5mm tips in ALL DIFFERENT COLOURS, which is impossible because they only do them in 10 colours in 0.4mm, and these 20 were all ones I'd never seen before in my life, like they had actually come direct from Japan, which they had because all the writing was in Japanese.

So I was just thinking which colours I would keep for me and which ones I would give to Nicola, or if we should take turns to pick, and then I reached in and there was another one exactly the same for her, like this woman had read my mind and we could have one each.

Then there were some notebooks from America, not fancy or anything, just really special. And make-up, which I don't really do, but this was the kind of thing that people don't really notice when you put it on, except yourself, like lipgloss and mascara and a little pot of gold glitter for parties, except for the bright purple nail varnish for my toes, because no-one sees it except in gym.

Everyone paints their toes except me. The whole thing made me so happy, it was like dreams I'd had. Not daydreams, real asleep dreams where I dream that I have a cupboard full of beautiful things then I wake up and it's not there.

Once, I dreamed that I had a cupboard full of beautiful umbrellas in lots of different colours, when I was a kid that was, and when I woke up I ran over to it and it just had my school clothes and some toys and books but no umbrellas of course. I was so upset I cried and it was a bit difficult to explain to my mother. So naturally enough I did have a strange feeling that I was about to wake up, but I didn't.

So all this time Unity was watching and commenting as well and I showed her it all and explained why it was really excellent to have it, and how it would help me to fit in a bit more at school and not feel like second class citizen. Just a few cool things like that, just to have them, something a bit different that wasn't old or cheap or not as good as anyone else's stuff.

Even if no one else noticed, that was going to make it better. Because it's not like I'm really materialistic or anything, because my dad always brought us up to value things that you can't just buy with money, but sometimes, even if you can't have it all, it's nice just to have one little bit of it, isn't it? If you've got nothing of it, and you wear glasses and

67

you are the school nerd, just one little thing can make it better. I explained this to Unity while we were going through all the lovely things and then she said,

"I think I can add something to the collection," smiling at me, "but first, how about a fresh fruit smoothie?"

CHAPTER TWELVE - JESSICA

When Unity came back she'd actually made us a smoothie in a blender, with fruit that she had in the fridge. I didn't know you could do that. I thought you had to buy them, so I didn't get them very often. She said I could try making my own with the £1 fruit baskets you can get from the stand outside the station, because mine was really delicious and she told me that she'd only used plums, a banana and an apple that she had handy.

Being with Unity was amazing. I suppose she was about the right age to be my aunt and I did wonder for a moment if she would consider adopting me, if you could do that with aunts.

"Unity," I said, "Do people come here just for you to be kind to them?"

"Well, Jessica. In a way you're right, they do," she said, "I do my best to be kind, but my visitors don't usually have a bag full of presents waiting for them; usually they just come to speak to me about things that are worrying them, because they'd like someone to listen to them and perhaps get a different viewpoint."

"I see." I said. "Which is probably why it says on the card that you solve problems. Shall I tell you about mine?"

"If you'd like to tell me about them, then I'd be happy to listen," she said, "What's bothering you?"

"My problem is this. I don't fit in I never have and I don't suppose I ever will," I said to her, "and I wasn't saying that to get sympathy, just because it's true and I'm not sure if I can sort it out because it's been like that ever since I can remember. But I did think that when my parents were married that I'd got two people I could count on to be on my side against the world, and now they're so busy being against each other that I don't even have that any more.

"And I used to be the odd one out at my old school because I was a bit good at science and no good at dancing, but I got away with it because I had some friends from when I was little, and I could mostly join in with all the things that everyone did. Now it's worse because my friends went to other schools and I can't do any of the things that cost a lot. And everyone has to have someone to pick on, and so mostly it's me, and to be honest, Unity, it does get me down a bit."

"I can understand that," she said, but looking at her, in this lovely room, with all her nice things and smiling at me, I wasn't sure that I believed her and I don't like to be rude but I had to know where I stood.

"Do you really?" I asked her, "Because you don't look as if you know what it's like to be in my situation. If you don't mind me commenting."

"No, I don't mind at all," she said, "That's a fair point, Jessica, so I'll explain something to you. When I was at school, we moved to a different area, and although my parents stayed married, I lost all my friends and my mother had to give up her job through being unwell. I didn't fit in either, and I didn't have the right uniform, just my old ones adapted to try to fit in with the new place. Plus I was quite good at passing exams and people sometimes hate that, don't they?"

She looked a bit sad when she talked about this, worse than me in fact.

"I see," I said. "I just wanted to check. How long does it last though? When do you start to feel as if you're not an outcast? Well not an outcast, exactly, but the odd one out, anyway."

"For me," she said, "It was university when I started to feel that I was relatively normal. Everyone was new and we all had to start again at the beginning, and I was no longer the brightest penny in the purse. There were people who were brilliant in every subject, a great deal wiser and more knowledgeable than me in every topic that you could think of. I could disappear into the mixture, blend in and find a place to fit.

There were still loads of cool, bitchy girls, but the place was large enough to avoid them. There are cool bitchy girls everywhere, by the way, but they calm down and become less influential the older you get, and some of them turn out rather well in the end…"

I pictured Emma Barker, Shirin Gupta and Natalie Ravenscroft-Price and I couldn't imagine that happening to them, but I didn't think I would argue.

"…even though you might find that quite hard to believe at the moment," said Unity, and I wondered if she had a secret way of reading my mind. "Experience and observation," she added, "That's how I do it. But for now, Jessica, what would you like to change?"

"I'd like my dad back," I said. "But I'm not sure I can do much about that. He's not dead or anything - that would be stupid - just divorced and sent away to suffer, my mother says."

"Tell me a bit about the situation, would you? Just to give me a general idea."

I told her as much as I knew really which was that I think things used to be fine, then my dad got this job which meant that he spent lots of time away. He was in charge of the engineering division in EMEA which I explained was short for Europe Middle East Africa. As his American bosses had decided that EMEA was the same size as America, he'd been travelling loads and my mother was always cross with him when he got home.

This went on for about two years, but sometimes they stopped arguing a bit and it was all OK again. But you never knew what it was going to be like when you came back from school so that was a bit stressful. Then he went to live somewhere else in a flat a mile away from us and my mother said they were getting a divorce.

I think my little brothers took it worse than me because dad used to play with them more, but when he was around he always had ideas for my homework. My mum did too, but mostly she's too busy to think about it because she's the one who's in charge of running the entire establishment, she says.

Sometimes we have her brother to stay, my Uncle Cormac. Partly he lives in Ireland but he comes here to work. He's quite good fun, but he and my mother just shut themselves away and plot stuff and are horrible about my dad and it doesn't really help.

Anyway, then it went from bad to worse, because at least we used to have holidays to look forward to. We'd all get in the car and drive over to France or go up to Scotland and go to the seaside and even if it rained there would be castles to visit and books to read.

So now we won't have the money for holidays, or anything really, except paying for essentials, mum said, because dad was stupid and had to buy a flat that we can only stay at sometimes, and less often than we're supposed to because my mum always argues about it, so officially he gets my brothers one weekend and me on the next, now his EMEA project is over and he's back in London again developing something, he says.

"So to sum up," I said, "I don't think that there's much I can do, is there? Except perhaps wait for university."

"Mmm, I don't know," said Unity, "It doesn't sound completely hopeless. Are either of them seeing anyone else, that you know about?"

"I think that was the problem at first," I said, "My dad had a girlfriend, and my mum found out about it, but by the time they split up it was all over, and then it was too late and my mum wasn't going to let him off that easily, she said.

I don't think my mum has a boyfriend or anything, but I don't know if maybe she goes out with anyone while we're at school, but she seems to spend most of her time with her friends and Uncle Cormac and Auntie Claire just talking about how useless men are and how you can't trust people and how it's stupid to fall in love because everyone will let you down."

"And do you believe that?" asked Unity.

"Oh no," I said, "I think that you've got to see the best in people, and encourage them to live up to it."

"Good-oh! And where do you get that from?" Unity asked me.

"I learned it from my gran, my dad's mother," I said, "And she was my favourite person but she died of a bad heart. That is to say it was very kind but it wasn't very strong. But I think she was right, and she was the happiest person that I know, and the nicest person to be with, so I would like to be like her, if possible, even though she left school without any qualifications and worked in a cake shop."

Unity looked as if I'd said something funny, but I was only telling her the truth, and she didn't laugh, she just smiled at me and said that my gran sounded wonderful and what a pity she wasn't still there for me to talk to, and I said that I thought that too.

"I've a couple of suggestions for you," she said, "I'd recommend that you have a go at keeping your mother away from the friends and family who encourage her to be disappointed in her fellow human beings, and find a way to have her spend time with people who have a slightly more positive view, people like you, for example. And perhaps you could suggest a day out one weekend, with your dad too. Get a family ticket for the tube, visit a place you'll all enjoy going, take a picnic maybe, and make them promise in advance that they won't argue. Tell them that your brothers need to see the whole family together. What have you got to lose?"

"It could only ruin one weekend, and maybe the rest of my life..." I said, just making a little joke, "but I'd like to have a go at it. I really would, even if I think it's going to be quite hard."

"You can't make people do what you want, or make everything turn out just right," Unity said, "But you do have an influence, and there's no point sitting back and watching everything go wrong, is there?"

"I think you're right," I said, "Is it wrong to think that it'll be easier now I have the right shoes for the job?" She laughed out loud.

"I did say that I had something else to add to your collection, didn't I?" she said. "I haven't forgotten, but I need your help. Close your eyes for a moment and picture a place where you fit in and you're feeling happy, then tell me where you are."

"I'm on my holidays, by the seaside in the west of Scotland, and I'm talking to a nice boy who likes me because we can say stuff about things we have in common, and I can stay there for as long as I like and go for long walks on the sand."

"I'll be right back," Unity said, got up, stretched her legs a bit, and walked out, looking back and smiling me at me as she left the room. I looked out of the window at the blackbird sitting on a tree branch. He looked as if he was staring right at me so I gave him a good stare back and smiled. I forgot about him when Unity came back with a little bottle.

"Perfume for you," she said.

"I don't really wear perfume," I said, "I wouldn't want you to waste it on me."

"Humour me," she said, "Just give it a little try." So I put it bit on my wrist like you do. It was amazing; it wasn't really perfume. All the others I'd smelled were like different flavours of bubble gum, and whoever wore them at school, just to see if they could get away with it, got them confiscated and got reported. This wasn't like them at all. What it smelled like was what you smell like after a day the beach in Scotland!

"That's not really perfume though," I said.

"Do you like it?" Unity asked.

"Of course I do! It's brilliant." I said. "It smells like the beach, not like bubblegum."

"Exactly," she said. "It's special perfume; do you think you could get away with wearing a little bit at school, without anyone noticing?" I said that I thought I probably could.

"Go ahead and wear it whenever you feel as though you're all alone, and it'll remind you that there are people here who are thinking of you: me, the lady on the bus, and your mum and dad when they get a moment."

"If I run out, am I allowed to come back and get a bit more?" I said.

"Jessica, you can come back here as often as you like," she said, and when I left I had a little card in my pocket to remind me of the time and date for our next meeting. Not that I would forget.

CHAPTER THIRTEEN - MARIANNE

I'd been feeling marvellous, on top of the world. It seemed as though I still enjoyed all the security and luxuries that my predictable husband brought me, with the added benefits of a new, interesting man who came home in time to spend the evening with us. In the afternoon, after my yoga class when I'd showered and dressed, I'd give myself a little dab of my roses to remind myself that things weren't so bad.

During a quiet evening in, after a glass or two of wine, I'd even told David about my trip into town which ended in my meeting Unity. He stayed very calm, and I told it in my best, self-deprecating, funny story way to see if I could get him to see the amusing side of my stalking him. Fortunately he laughed; he even seemed a little pleased that I'd gone to all that trouble to find out whether or not he was seeing someone else.

But I did have a little problem, and it was about reprioritising. I used to spend time with Josie after yoga; we'd always have a coffee or two, and a quick dry white if there was an after school club or something to keep our kids occupied.

I felt badly about deserting her, especially since her divorce, but she made me feel guilty about being happily married – again – and I was having to pretend that I envied her her freedom. So I cut her to down to once a week and stopped joining in with the character assassination of her ex-husband (and felt terrible about how enthusiastically I used to criticise my own).

I got the impression she thought I'd become rather self-righteous and judgemental. I didn't mean to, but while I'd never felt entirely comfortable in the black humour of broken marriages, Josie was terribly witty and amusing and always entertaining to spend time with.

The other thing was that she was awfully short of cash, because although she'd got herself the family home, her ex-husband didn't have the money to support two households, so I was always the one who always bought the drinks. It seemed mean to give it up.

But all the same, I cut our meetings back and instead I'd go home to meet David. She obviously felt that I'd betrayed her, if that's not too strong a word, and made a fool of her (or myself) by playing the faithful wife again.

So I was most definitely not expecting her brother show up on my doorstep one morning when I'd just got back from the grocery shopping. He'd brought me a rather odd gift which he said he couldn't resist buying - just a packet of biscuits with ginger and chocolate - and he asked if he could come in for a coffee to eat them with me.

It was all a bit strange, but what do you do? Tell a man that he can't come in, accept the gift and shut the door, or announce that you don't have time for him and his biscuits. It was all too bizarre, so I became completely spineless and politely British and let him in.

I'm not proud of this, and I don't completely understand it myself, but I think that my issues were not all resolved by one trip to Paris, one to 25 Bloomsbury Mews and the smell of roses. Can you get rid of several accumulated years of boredom and complacency in a couple of weeks? Perhaps not.

I'm not trying to excuse myself, just to explain myself. Mack followed me into the kitchen and stood very close to me. The first time we'd met, I was almost certain that Josie had sold her brother on the idea of me as a potential candidate for patching up his hurt heart. A minor flirtatious distraction. A frustrated suburban housewife for the use of. She probably thought she was doing me a favour, introducing me to her handsome younger brother.

We had some coffee and ate a couple of biscuits, standing in my beautifully remodelled kitchen, then when he put his hands on my shoulders I didn't do what I ought to have done. I just stayed there. It was absolutely stupid. I was absolutely stupid.

I steered him to the spare room; there's a limit to my faithlessness. I wasn't going to allow the man in my bedroom, but somehow I lacked the power – or the inclination - to stop. It was exciting and wonderful and new while it was happening. Then it turned into a complete nightmare, right at the moment he left. What on earth? I showered, I washed the bedclothes, and I washed the coffee cups and put the biscuits in the bird-feeder in the garden. I decided that it hadn't happened. I felt as though a friend had died and that I'd never see her again. I was cold and shaking, so I had a cup of tea and some Marmite on toast.

I opened my handbag, scrambled about in it to find my bottled roses and covered myself in the scent; breathing it calmed me. Then it reminded me of the project I'd been working on with Unity, and just how badly I had gone off the rails.

The girls got in and disappeared into their room after a cursory greeting. When David came home, I threw myself into his arms.

"You smell good," he said and then he saw my face, "Had a bad day?"

I looked at him and his honest, trusting expression and that was the point at which I decided to lie my head off.

"I think I've got a bit of a chill," I said, "So I skipped yoga and just hung around here."

"I'll go out and grab some food," he said, "Pizza OK?" and he got changed out of his suit into his jeans and sweatshirt, wrapped up in his padded jacket and disappeared off to the local organic place on his newly rediscovered bike.

I got through the evening and went off to bed early. I wasn't asleep when David got to bed, but he just kissed me on the forehead and nodded off. I lay there half way between the shame of it and the delight of how marvellously exciting it had been.

My appointment with Unity was the next day. And to think I'd almost given it to Josie. I couldn't eat breakfast; I had a cup of tea and was about to leave the house, smelling of roses, when the doorbell rang. I don't know what I was expecting, but I wasn't expecting to see him on my doorstep. He was carrying a bunch of flowers and looking up at me with puppy eyes, the way Diana Princess of Wales used to do when she wanted the nation to feel sorry for her.

"I'm going out," I said, grabbed my bag and shut the door behind me. "And what the hell are you doing here?" I asked in a hissy whisper in case the neighbours were in hearing distance, but come to think of it that probably would have made them listen harder. I moved swiftly down the garden path and he followed me.

"You didn't think I was just going to walk away and leave, did you?" he said, "I'm too much of a gentleman."

I opened the gate, speechless for the moment. I hadn't taken time to think any of this through. I was expecting to consign him to the past but apparently he already had plans for our future.

"A gentleman?" I said, walking quickly along the street with him at my side, keeping up, "One who seduces married women?"

"Married women?" he said, sounding mildly offended? "I don't make a habit of it. You're my first."

I stopped at the corner of our road, before it joined the busier one where my friends might spot me with a man holding a bunch of green pom-pom dahlias. Part of me wanted to lead him back to the house, and part of me wanted to slap his audacious face, but the larger part of me just wanted him to go away and leave me alone for ever. So I wanted to make this clear before I got on the bus and headed into town. To myself, mostly.

"Look. I know I was just as happy as you were to go along with this yesterday, but I don't know what I was thinking. I made a dreadful mistake, and I never want to do this again. Can you please respect that? I don't want to see you again," I said, not very calmly.

"Are you certain about that?" he said, smiling in his charming way, "Because yesterday, I could have sworn that you and I had a great time." I felt as if I was going to faint. It was horrifying; he could have told Josie, he might tell David; everything about this was disastrous. I had learned something, quickly and with absolute certainty: I did not want to give up my husband and my life; the idea terrified me. I had to sit down on the nearest garden wall.

"I'm certain," I said, "I actually am absolutely certain about this. Please forget it ever happened."

"You look dreadful," he said, "Let me buy you a coffee," and he sat down on the wall beside me. I stood up and headed for the stop just as the bus swung around the corner. I got straight on. I looked back and saw him smiling sadly at me, his head tilted sideways. Was it sadness or was it emotional manipulation? I don't know.

But I do know people like him. They can go either way at an unstable moment like that; they can either meet a woman, fall in love and calm down, or they can create chaos. So I was his first married woman, was I? I hoped I hadn't helped him to choose chaos, because if he had, I felt sorry for the women who were about to be part of his quest. Those men always have a quest.

In Bloomsbury, I called at the coffee shop because by then I was hungry. I had myself a chocolate muffin and a cappuccino and was feeling a lot better by the time I walked up to the black door and rang the bell. Carl's handsome, smiling face greeted me, and I noticed that he'd had some navy blue added to his dreads.

He smelled like a walk through the woods in autumn.

As soon as I sat down with Unity I started to cry. She gave me a beautifully laundered handkerchief.

"That bad?" she said. She made tea then sat quietly until I had calmed down enough to talk.

"I don't do this all the time, you know," I said, still snivelling a bit, "Just when I'm here." I laughed a little but my eyes ached and my head hurt.

"Do you want to tell me?" she said, and so I did. I told her the whole thing, and when I'd finished we just sat for a while.

"This is going to sound like rather a trivial question," she said, "so please try not to yell at me, but were you wearing the rose scent at the time?"

"No," I said, "No I wasn't. I hadn't got around to putting it on. It's usually an afternoon thing after I've done all my chores, as a reward. Why?"

"For me, it's important to know if it still makes you feel comfortable," she said, so I sniffed my wrists and thought about it.

"It's interesting," I said, "It makes me feel as though I made the right decision running away this morning. It's OK. It's still all mine. Although I might forever associate it with a strange time in my life."

"In that case, we might move you on to another one," she said, "we'll see how it all works out."

"I can't believe it'll ever work out," I said, "Not from where I'm sitting, not at the moment. For a start, how am I going to explain it to David. Will he forgive me? What if he throws me out?"

"Have you considered not telling him at all?" she said, to my total astonishment, "You might consider what good it could possibly do."

"Yes, well I suppose I'm already part of the way down that path. I lied by omission last night. But I thought that honesty was essential in relationships," I said, "Surely I have to tell him in order to move on."

"You've already moved on, haven't you?" Unity said, "You've assessed what you did, discovered that you made a mistake, and from what you've told me, it's helped you to appreciate what you have, and to stop wondering if the alternatives are worth trying."

"And what if I get found out?" I said, "What if he tells his sister and she spreads it around our entire community?"

"Deny it!" said Unity. "His word against yours. He came over, tried to kiss you, you fought him off and he started the rumours because his feelings were hurt. You didn't say anything because you were so ashamed. Besides, he might never say anything precisely because you've rejected him. His charms are not completely irresistible, are they? He won't want that broadcast."

I started to cheer up a bit.

"Oh my goodness," I said, "That's really dreadful but brilliant. But then I'll have to lie to my husband for ever."

"It's either that or you make him miserable," she said. "What's the kindest thing to do? Make yourself feel better by sharing your guilt and hurting him more than you can imagine, or absorbing it yourself? Victorian codes of morality can be over-rated."

I was stunned. It hadn't occurred to me that keeping it to myself might be the ethical thing to do. I couldn't take it back, but I could bury it. That way, I would be punished for my badness but David would not. I wondered, was I kidding myself? Did he have a right to be told? I honestly didn't know, but I didn't feel compelled to confess. Before I left, Unity disappeared up the creaking stairs again and came back with a blue bottle for me.

"Try this," she said.

It was roses again, but different. My original was like being wrapped in a pink fluffy blanket of softness, but this one was like opening the door and stepping out on a spring morning, full of brightness and light.

"Who'd have thought that roses could be so unlike each other?" I said.

"Yes. Who'd have thought?" she said, and smiled.

CHAPTER FOURTEEN - GRACE

It was time for our annual reviews. Alice was first. She was in David's office for almost an hour and frankly I wondered what they could think of to talk about. She's done exactly the same job for the last ten years, as far as I can see. She seemed pleased when she got out, and then it was my turn. I had a few things to say to David, but I'd decided to allow him to feel as though he was in control.

I'd been dumped by the man I'd been cultivating for the previous three years, but if that meant I ought to be concentrating on a career for a while, then so be it.

After all, with a decade of child-bearing years left in me I had time to land myself another decent fish! There are plenty in the ocean, particularly when you're an attractive piece of bait in a very large pond. Goodness, that sounded awful! What a dreadful metaphor; I got quite carried away.

But let's face it, I'm not a bad catch. I'm fit and trim, intelligent and capable, and to be perfectly honest Daddy did not like Cormac, although Mummy did! (I've never met a woman who doesn't, which was part of the problem.) I'm certain that Daddy would have done his best to make sure my intended didn't get his hands on any of our money, just in case he wandered off, but he was content as long as his little angel was happy.

Daddy had heard a rumour that my fiancé wasn't entirely committed to our relationship, although he didn't tell me until after it ended. One of his associates who'd attended our engagement party had seen someone he was certain was Cormac behaving as if he were intimate with a woman from his office, so to speak, in a pub in Shepherd's Market.

We were engaged, we'd talked about setting a date, Daddy had given me a budget for a larger flat in town and I'd been looking for suitable places. We met on a Friday evening and I handed him a sheaf of papers: 16 possible homes ranging from bijou in Knightsbridge to a good deal larger in Chiswick. That was when he told me "it's not you, it's me" and that he wasn't ready to settle down after all. At the age of 42, I ask you! Not ready.

I couldn't eat for a week, then I went out to Kent for a weekend with Mummy and Daddy, got some fresh air, got him off my mind for a while, and met some of my old friends and realised that I was probably better sticking to someone from my own social group. A branch of his family had some land and he did have connections, but most of them were in Ireland so one simply didn't know them.

I'd met him through a friend of a friend who worked at the same company, something in communications technology, slightly modern, perhaps a little unstable for someone on whom one wished to build one's future prosperity.

Of course I told everyone that I'd been the one to end it, Frankly though, if he would realise how stupid he had been, beg me with sufficient humility to accept him – on my own terms – as his fiancée once again, then I'd be back in his arms in a flash.

Since my engagement ended, I'd wondered if perhaps being a PA wasn't sufficiently challenging. I could develop a new niche for myself, then exaggerate my responsibilities, update my CV and move on to a larger company. That would increase my chances of finding a more suitable marriage candidate. Perhaps public relations could become my forté. I could see myself as a professional PR, speaking to the press, handling events, which I already did anyway, sometimes.

Also, I toyed with the idea of rescuing David from his patently shambolic marriage, although I'm not certain that Daddy would have wanted me to take up with a married man, certainly not until he'd left his wife. However, David had been behaving oddly, going home on time but also slipping out occasionally to meetings that weren't in his diary, just blanked out so that neither of us could book in any appointments.

Perhaps someone had pipped me at the post.

He invited me in. We talked about how the business was getting along then we discussed the printing market and the tricky situation with overseas competition and online publishing – that was mostly David - then he surprised me by asking what my plans were.

I told him that I was thinking that I might do a bit of PR and he asked to enlarge upon what my ideas were for the company! I hadn't actually got as far as thinking it through so I just waffled a little until I ran out of steam, feeling slightly ridiculous. I'd been expecting to demand a PR position and more money; instead I was starting to feel as though I had to justify my existence. Alice, he explained, had asked for permission to develop our social media strategy! (What a bitch; she'd never said a thing about it.)

David had always taken a slight interest in our personal lives; in an office of three we kept each other up to date, although we didn't ever stray into the realms of gossip or speculation. Of course he knew that my engagement had ended. He'd kindly taken me to lunch several times, and I'd felt at the time that there was an opportunity to take it further had I wished.

I know my strengths. I did do a spot of modelling after college and I know how to make the best of my assets, without crossing a line into anything which could possibly be construed as overtly sexual. That was how I bagged the Irishman in the first place. I wanted someone with good genes; that was rather more important than money. The last thing I wanted was some short-sighted, paunchy chap looking for a strapping lass to bear him an heir.

Oh well, not David then, but who?

He asked me how I was feeling. Feeling? I didn't know. Was it possible that Cormac and I would overcome our problems? Could the wedding be back on? I hadn't been expecting this and I found that I was unable to reply. David quickly changed the subject and we went back to talking about my taking on a PR role. But then I felt a little down.

It hadn't worked out the way I'd planned and I couldn't help feeling that it was mostly my own fault. If you want something to work out the way you plan it, you have to do rather more planning. Did I really want any of this? What did I want? I started to feel that life was a complete waste of time. David could obviously see it in my face.

"Grace," he said, "I think that you deserve a break, in both senses of the word. You've been through a lot this year and you haven't given yourself time to recover. I'd like you to take a month to decide what it is you want to do. Write me a PR plan. Include all the things you think we ought to do to help our company become more successful. Go skydiving, white water rafting, ballet dancing, I don't mind. But come back in a month and tell me what you really want."

Then he handed me a card. Written on it was an address, a date and a time and a suggestion that someone would solve my problems. That, I doubted.

It was almost time to leave, so I picked up my most important belongings, packed them in the spare eco-shopper I kept in my bottom drawer (La Grande Epicerie de Paris, obviously, not Tesco) and just walked out. I didn't feel capable of explaining to Alice, suddenly finding myself a little tearful as I was shutting down my desktop. So off I went.

Back at my flat, in one of the nicer 1930s Chelsea modernist blocks, I had a cup of tea and a think, something I'd been avoiding for a month or two - thinking, not tea.

Obviously I missed Cormac terribly. I lay awake at night, reading until I fell asleep with a book on my head. If I closed my eyes and waited for sweet dreams to arrive, I'd just stay wide awake imagining stupid things, like the phone ringing and having him tell me what a dreadful mistake he'd made and begging me to come back to him.

They do say that after six months the men who dump you suddenly call you and do just that, but by then most women have moved on. Actually, they call you because the woman they left you for has turned out to be not so marvellous after all. Let's face it, they usually leave you for someone else.

Women leave men to get their lives back; men leave women for someone younger. That's what mummy told me. I've always admired the way she has managed to hang on to daddy for all these years.

So, as I said, I found myself at home in Chelsea, on my own I astonished and humiliated myself by bursting into tears and sobbing until my eyes hurt. I was lonely, and furious for allowing this to happen. Irrational, I know. I'd planned to find a husband, met a few for whom I could have "settled", but hadn't because I knew I could do better.

Then I found Cormac, a man so phenomenally good looking that he turned heads as he passed. I could have had a career, but frankly all my efforts were put into making myself a decent match! Now what? A wasteland. No suitors lining up for my attention and no-one in my life who could compare with the one I'd allowed to get away. So perhaps I did have a problem.

That week, several times, I came within a smidgen of picking up the phone and calling him, but instead I called my friends, and went out for a quick drink or an emergency bout of mercy shopping. The only way to restore a relationship after a broken engagement was to return triumphant with a wedding date in the diary, in ink. I hate to sound cynical or old-fashioned, but if you want commitment from a man who has proven himself indecisive, you have to make it legal.

The following week, I'd got nowhere with the PR plans. Too much time spent distracting myself with wayward "what if?s" and waiting for his call. If he didn't call, how could I negotiate? Then it occurred to me that he might never call again. That struck me so hard that I felt as if my body had been hollowed out and filled with ice. I cried more, but this wasn't a short, noisy sobbing fit; my tears flowed slowly all evening.

So, to cut a long story short, I decided that I could do worse than spend an hour in the company of the person who solves problems. I took a taxi because it's pleasant to travel above ground.

The driver chatted away about Chelsea, idiotically assuming that I was interested in the football team because I lived in the area, then he dropped me outside a black door, managed to turn around in the mews avoiding the parked bicycles and the Porsche over the road and rattled off over the cobbles.

The black door had been painted over and over until it had lost all its detail and become sleek and almost animal-like as it shone in the sun. Any decent decorator would have had it stripped down to the wood and brought back to its original condition. It was one of those properties that are merely maintained, rather than invested in.

Only the poor and the seriously aristocratic took that kind of risk with their buildings, usually because they didn't have the cash handy to keep up everything up to standard. As it was unlikely that a problem-solving outfit was run by an Anglo-Norman family, I wasn't certain that it was for me, and was expecting to see an inadequately dressed business person invite me in.

Instead, I found myself facing an expanse of tightly clad chest, constrained by a fine cotton t-shirt in plain sea green, and leading to a kind smiling face further embellished with blue-streaked dreadlocks. What a turn-up for the books! The day started to look even brighter.

"Carl" he said, offering me his large but surprisingly elegant hand.

"Grace," I answered back. He smiled as I walked in, closing the door by reaching easily over my head, and turning to lead the way. I mused as I walked after him as to the effect that taking a tall, handsome black chap home might have on mummy and daddy. I was certain that mummy would get over it in a moment. As for daddy, it would rather depend on his financial status.

If he was intending to solve my problems then I was most definitely interested. I wasn't sure whether the aroma in the hallway came from the ages old wooden structure or the man himself, or a blend of the two, but the smell of treading on bracken and branches out in the woods made me nostalgic for the countryside.

He guided me to an office, or consulting room, I suppose it was. It was light, with a view of the sunshine on a lovely, but tiny, garden. Tiny compared to our home, of course. For the middle of London, it was remarkably generous. I could smell the end of autumn through the window and paused to look at the backs of the tall, Georgian houses behind the trees, huge places that I supposed now belonged to the university or solicitors or private members' clubs.

I turned to ask him where to sit and he'd disappeared.

There were two quite decent Victorian wing chairs, upholstered à la mode in amusingly bright modern velvets, and two modernist black leather classic psychiatrists' couches. One looked sufficiently beaten up to be original Bauhaus, and the other was probably a copy. There was absolutely no way that I would be invitingly draping myself over one of those in front of the tall dark handsome stranger so I chose a wing chair, which bounced pleasingly when I sat on it.

My disappointment must have been all too painfully obvious when the door opened and a small, older woman with uncontrollable hair and archaic make-up showed up instead, sliding into the room rather apologetically. Good shoes though. I waited for her to explain how long I'd have to wait before Carl came back.

"Grace," she said, "I'm Unity," and she sat down. That was really quite irritating. I had a man to catch

CHAPTER FIFTEEN - GRACE

"Do you know what it is we do here?" Unity asked me.

"You solve problems," I said.

"Absolutely," she said, ignoring my sarcasm, or not noticing. She smiled and I noticed that I was smiling back. She had infected me with it. "Would you like to tell me how you came to be here?"

"You first," I said. "I'd like to know what your qualifications are before I commit to an arrangement, and I'd like a confidentiality agreement."

She smiled again, leaned forward in her matching wing chair and asked, "Who introduced you to us?"

"It was David Cavendish."

"Do you trust him?"

"Of course I do."

"If you feel that you need more than a personal recommendation from David Cavendish, then we're not the right people for you," she said, cornering me nicely, "and if you don't feel comfortable here, you'd be better off finding someone who's more up your street."

Up your street. I remember her using that phrase, which seemed curiously down to earth for such unusual surroundings. Did I feel comfortable? I didn't respond straight away. I thought about the place. Slightly shabby, but nothing tawdry about it. She seemed educated, which I supposed was something to be hoped for in a problem solver. She wasn't of my background, but I couldn't pin down where she actually did originate. As for Carl, what was he exactly? The butler? Comfortable. The chair was comfortable, the room was warm enough, and Unity herself had a presence that was unexpectedly reassuring. I felt as though she wasn't rushing to judge me nor was she jealous, which women often are.

"Yes, I do feel comfortable," I said. "I'll stay if you don't mind." Then Carl came in with a tray: tea and cakes, served in old, worn but unchipped china. I accepted a cup of tea and helped myself to a cake with pink icing, then he left. She caught me appraising his form as he walked out and she smiled and raised her eyebrows. So was he the husband, gay best friend, colleague? No idea. She had begun to amuse me and besides, there was cake.

"I'll tell you, then," I said, "And let's see what you can do." And over the brim of a cup of tea I watched her curl back into her armchair ready for storytime.

"I work for David Cavendish. I've been there for five years and I have used my job as a way to pass the time between social events at which I could build my contact list, fill my address book, meet suitable men and prepare for the future." I paused for effect.

"How do you see your future panning out?" she said, annoyingly cutting in.

"Well, I don't have to worry about money," I said, looking – I hoped – satisfied but not arrogant, "but I'm the only child of a wealthy businessman, and I'd like to spend my days perpetuating our family, supporting my husband in his endeavours and, although this might sound old fashioned – running the perfect household. I would like to be featured in *House & Garden*." I saw her glance at my left hand where there was still a slight mark from the engagement ring.

"And no, I don't yet actually have a husband." Oh, the horror; I started to weep silent tears. Unity produced a clean white cotton handkerchief and went up in my estimation.

"That," she said, "would definitely put a spanner in the works."

Despite myself, I laughed a little; we sat, sipped tea and I sniffed unappealingly, and after a while I was ready to talk.

"I was engaged until recently." I said, "I broke it off. No, what's the point in lying to you? He broke it off. We were house-hunting and he had one of those male panics about not settling down yet. I told all my friends it was me, because I couldn't bear it. All the fuss I'd made about it, the engagement party, planning the wedding, then I pretended I'd got carried away in the event and had forgotten that Cormac wasn't the right man for me."

"What's his name?" asked Unity, leaning forwards slightly.

"Yes, it's an unusual one," I said, spelling it for her, "It's Irish."

"I see," she said and merged with her chair once again.

"So I'm torn," I said, "Between waiting to see if he comes back, which apparently they can do after about six months, suddenly declaring their undying love, saying how much they missed you, offering to marry you the next day and have as many children as you like. And the other thing, which is to get right out there and look for a better one.

"Daddy didn't like him, you see, and daddy is a good judge of character. It was daddy who heard that Cormac had been seen with another woman; you just can't do that in London without someone spotting you, you know? It's not six degrees of separation here; it's more like one-and-a-half."

"But you would have married him, if he hadn't called it off?" she asked.

"Daddy would have come round," I said, "But I'm not certain that he would now." I paused. "That's an interesting thought, Unity. If he did get down on his knees and beg me to be his wife, he would still have to convince daddy that he was worthy, and at the moment I think that particular hurdle is a little too high for him."

"Did he give you a reason?" Unity asked me.

"He said he wasn't ready," I replied, "Just not ready. Very sorry. Perhaps we could continue to "see each other" which means sex with no strings, of course, so I said absolutely not! I have my standards... But sometimes I wish I didn't."

She smiled.

"Is he as attractive as you are beautiful?" she asked?

"Absolutely he is!" I said, "Which is part of the problem. With a man that good looking, one is always concerned that someone will try to steal him away."

"Or that he will use his good looks to flatter and seduce?" she asked.

"I hardly think so!" I said, but I started to wonder. "Why do you ask?"

"You said he told you he wasn't ready," she said slowly and seriously. "And in my experience - which is limited of course, so excuse my conjecture – people who leave are often interested in exploring the sexual options which are available to them at the time. People who have affairs which they regret, and which are discovered, then ask for forgiveness and to be allowed to put everything back the way it was. Cormac is behaving like an explorer."

I thought. Unity poured tea.

"There was something that worried me at the time," I said. "It was his sister. We never met, but from what he said she seemed to be frantically anti-marriage. She was hounding him rather, to make hay while the sun shines. Her husband had had an affair, which has since ended badly, and I got the impression that she was seeing someone on the side too. Heavens, perhaps I'm best away from the whole family.

"It wasn't that she objected to me, as such, but she objected to anyone who was going to clip her little brother's wings. Each time he visited her, he was distracted and unfocused, irritated by things I did which didn't normally irritate him. Do you think she put him up to it?"

"I don't know," said Unity," Do you?"

"Aren't you the one who's supposed to solve the problems?" I asked, perhaps a trifle unkindly.

"I need more information first," she said, unperturbed and added, "Would you take him back?"

"I would at bedtime!" I declared, and sniggered like a schoolgirl.

"Have another cake," said Unity with a grin. Dammit, I was starting to like the woman.

"Daytime?" she asked.

"I know what would happen," I said after a while. "I wouldn't trust him. Daddy had affairs, you know? But he was discreet and I think he's stopped now. Too old for the bother and too rich to take the risk of a stray baby and maintenance for life. Does that sound hard? But Daddy stayed put. You can pretend it hasn't happened if you stay put.

"I'm not saying it was right, and of course mummy was hurt, but she won. And I don't think they really bothered, you know, after a couple of decades of marriage, so she was pleased not to have to submit to his demands. Cormac left me. I want someone who loves me too much ever, ever to do that."

"Too damn right!" said Unity, surprising me.

"But where shall I find him? I look around and everyone seems so pale and dull compared to Cormac. Do I sound sorry for myself?"

"I understand," she said. "But perhaps you could stop looking for a while, just to give yourself a chance to get your thoughts in order. Concentrate on your work perhaps?"

"Did David tell you to say that?" I asked, miffed.

"Be fair, Grace. He didn't even know you'd turn up."

"I suppose," I said, "I did think of doing the company's PR, but to be honest, I was too distracted to concentrate. I could try harder."

"Why don't you sign up for a course?" she said, "Amuse yourself. Sometimes when you stop looking, what you're looking for finds you."

"Oh, don't be ridiculous!" I said, "You sound like my mother's new age chakra-balancing crystal therapist. But I'll go on a course. What is there to lose but precious hours that I could spend on blind dates? I've no time to waste, you know. Clock ticking."

"Then you are opening yourself up to misuse," she said. "There are people who can sense desperation, are prepared to offer you a sniff of commitment. I need you to look for an equal, for balance, for someone who values you for who you are, not just how good you look together in his holiday photographs."

I pictured Cormac's online albums; he uploaded reams of photos of us on the beach in Mauritius earlier in the year; his friends posted salacious comments which he made no effort to delete. They were still there last time I looked. I'd taken it as a sign of hope, but perhaps I was only a trophy. I smudged my mascara on Unity's handkerchief as I started to cry again.

"But where do I find a nice man?" I whinged.

"You start by noticing that they are there," said Unity, "instead of screening them out as dull, soft or generally unsuitable before they've had a chance."

I continued to sniff.

"I want you to think for a moment," she said, taking advantage of my inability to string a sentence together. "Think back to a time when you were friends with a boy, or a man, really good friends, someone you didn't have to impress, someone for whom you had a deep affection, someone it would make you smile to see again."

So I thought. I just sat there and thought back to school days and remembered long evenings after school playing in the woods with my friends. It's the kind of thing that fills suburban parents with horror these days, but it was wonderful. We ran, we jumped, we climbed trees, we rode horses. We got muddy and wet and exhausted. We hid, we chased, we swung from ropes, we were exhilarated and excited and I've ever experienced anything as intensely pleasurable since. No really. I'd almost forgotten. I looked up to see Unity looking into me so deeply that I wondered if she could read my mind.

"I used to play with my friends in the woods." I said. "I was safe, because it was only at the end of our garden, over a small stream, into some land on the edge of my friend's farm. He was my junior school boyfriend when I was nine or ten. There were about eight of us. We'd meet up and just run about a lot.

"Kevin's dad, that was his name, my boyfriend, Kevin, I ask you. Well, his father had horses and we could ride them sometimes as long as we put the work in. We brushed the old nags until they gleamed and we polished their ancient saddles. I even plaited their manes and tails once.

"We'd have tea at someone's house and one mother would call to tell the other mothers she was cooking; then we would play until it was so dark we had to go home. You wouldn't think it to look at me now, but I don't think there's anything finer than swinging upside down from a tree branch."

I thought about what I was saying.

"How could I have forgotten all that?" I wondered out loud. "Marvellous times, filed away, like old photographs."

Unity was smiling. I could see her picturing it, more than that; she seemed to be feeling what I was feeling.

"What became of Kevin?" she asked.

"We just stopped," I said. "I was away at school, then I used to see him sometimes and get such a feeling of excitement, such a rush, then I suppose I fell for someone else and Kevin became less important until I forgot him completely.

"I saw him again though, when I was about 20. He was at agricultural college and I was studying something pointless and we seemed to have lost our way. His friends were all farmers, not the upper class sort, just the people who happen to have a few fields and a load of cows, and I was busy comparing the price of flats in Fulham and Putney and shopping for shoes. I just couldn't see myself in wellingtons and a dung-stained Barbour, getting up at five to jam a milking machine on a big, smelly animal."

"But you considered it at some time," Unity observed of my detailed description.

"Yes, I'd thought it through," I said, "But then again, daddy didn't encourage the relationship either. He hoped for more for me."

"More what?" she asked.

"More... socially, I suppose," I said.

"Because he thought that would make you happier than being married to your childhood sweetheart?"

I paused. I suppose that what daddy wanted, ultimately, was my happiness, but I did start to wonder if his motives were completely pure. Then again, were mine? I am a firm believer that money makes you happy, or at least that a lack of it can make you seriously unhappy.

But even though Kevin Newton's family never had a lot of money, I can't remember feeling more warm and content than when I was sitting at their long kitchen table, by a wood fire, eating Mrs Newton's mince pies after a game of hide and seek in their snow-covered woods.

"Oh bollocks!" I said, "You've made me reconsider my entire reason for being." I laughed out loud and I actually felt happy. And she joined in because it was infectious, or because she'd just heard me say bollocks.

"Your father will worry if you go doing things like that," Unity said, but I do think that in his heart of hearts he must want you to be truly content."

When I'd calmed down again I told her what I remembered. That I believed I'd had felt happiest with Kevin, aged ten, sitting in his mum's kitchen, by the fire, eating mince pies, warming up and drying out, then sitting on an ancient couch watching an equally ancient television until it was time to go home. We didn't ever kiss or hold hands or anything the slightest bit sexual; that would have been "soppy", but we were the best of friends and I do think we loved each other in a way that I've never managed since. No games, no point scoring, no power struggles. That's the way I'd like it to be.

"I'll just be a moment," Unity said and left the room. Carl came back in and cleared away the cups. I pondered their relationship again, but no longer felt the need to try to steal him. We just smiled at each other; there was a lot of smiling to be done in this odd little place. Quite a bit of crying too, but the smiles seemed to have it on points.

Then she was back, with a small bottle. Nothing expensive, just a plain blue bottle with a black lid. It looked ever so slightly unpleasantly medical, but I was wrong about that.

"Scent," she said, "See if you like it." So I sniffed then dabbed it on my neck.

"Oh lord!" I said and my knees went weak. Fortunately I was still sitting. I felt the tears threatening to spill over again. "It's Mrs Newton's kitchen at Christmas, isn't it? How did you do that?"

"Use it," she said, "to remind yourself that there are people who will treat you as an equal, who will love you – yes, for your looks and your money – but for yourself too, if you'll let them."

Then I left, and went home, and packed a weekend bag and took the train out to Surrey.

CHAPTER SIXTEEN - MARIANNE

I can't describe how much I was *not* looking forward to meeting Josie. I had no excuse for cancelling our Tuesday afternoon coffee-after-yoga session, so I was going to have to go through with it. I had help though; in class I smelled so strongly of roses that I thought the teacher might comment, then I topped myself up with another helping after my shower.

"Not you too?" Josie said as we sat down with our caffe lattes.

"Not me too what?" I asked, genuinely not understanding her question.

"Not you with your mysterious blue bottle of perfume too," said Josie, "What's that called? Granny's garden?" I smiled at her wit and I paused. To explain meant that I would be obliged to talk about meeting Unity, admitting to spying on David, and then deciding to change my attitude towards our marriage. That would mean a long conversation, to be greeted, I suspected, with Josie's scathing sarcasm, which until a few weeks ago I would have encouraged.

Fortunately, she didn't notice I'd not answered and continued,

"So did you find out more about the fancy woman? 'Brand Consultant' is it? A 23-year-old business studies graduate, is it?"

"You know what?" I said, aiming for a blend of self-deprecation and suspense, "I was completely wrong about her."

"Right," said Josie, not believing a word of it.

"It's true," I said with a smile, wanting to win her over without having to delve into the details. Then I laughed a little at the face she was pulling. The one that said, "He's spinning you a line and you've fallen for it. Well, we've all heard that one before, my darling."

"I've even met her," I said, missing out the how and why. "She's the one who gave me the scent."

"Jesus, Mary and Joseph," said Josie, "The whole world's smelling of roses," and laughed like a machine gun at her own joke. "Even my own daughter's wearing some kind of scent these days. Kids! The next thing

I know she'll be pregnant with triplets and I'll have to pay for them from the meagre allowance that skinflint pays me."

"Is it really over for good then?" I asked, distracting her back on to her favourite topic.

"Why would I want him back? Complete waste of space!" Josie said, picking up where we'd left off the previous week and many weeks before that, then she suddenly did a U-turn.

"But what about you? If it wasn't the 'brand consultant' creature, then who is it? His secretary? Are you going to wait until you catch him then sue him for every penny he has?"

She waited, smiling keenly, eyebrows raised ready for me to join in our usual speculations. I had an attack of nerves, a little squeeze of the stomach, the kind I only get these days before standing up to make an announcement at the PTA or when the girls go into a piano exam.

"I've been considering a different strategy," I said.

"Yes? What?"

"I'm considering keeping everything I already have, including David."

"What do you mean?" Josie looked astonished.

"I mean," I said, lowering my voice so that our classmates at the neighbouring tables wouldn't hear everything we said unless they tried very hard, which they appeared to be doing, "I've been counting my blessings. I thought about how I would feel if David really were having an affair, and I decided I'd hate it. That's all. There was a possibility that he was seeing someone else and I didn't like it one little bit.

"So," deep breath, "I went to see his brand consultant and I found out that she's real. She's not his mistress, she's a very nice woman, and she's helping to sort out our marriage. There's no affair, nothing happening, it was all in my imagination."

Josie sat back in her uncomfortable wrought iron café chair, tilted her head to one side, pursed her lips and folded her arms. It felt like school, when I'd just told the teacher something stupid.

"Well, there's a turn up for the books!" Josie said. She looked at me blandly, her as if she were trying to decide what to feel next, her normal animation all wiped away.

"Would that be why you rejected my brother after you were so obviously hitting it off?" she asked coldly.

I was so relieved I couldn't speak. He hadn't told her. One scrap of him was made of decent stuff. Not the bit that breaks off a relationship with his fiancée and not the bit that seduces a married woman, but the bit that keeps its mouth shut when it realises that nothing is to be gained from telling.

"Well, it's your loss," Josie said and her voice had resumed its flippant lightness, "Or so I understand," she added, "As I obviously have no idea what my own brother is like as a lover."

The conversation at the next table died down from a murmur to complete silence.

"Oh well," she said, "If you're going to disappear up your own backside, I shall have to get him back together with his snooty bitch of a fiancée. At least she's rich."

And that was it, over, for now at least. Josie continued to chastise and mock me for lacking a sense of adventure and for my pathetic faithfulness, all of which I gratefully accepted, water off a duck's back, as a much smaller punishment than I deserved.

CHAPTER SEVENTEEN - GRACE

I'd been back in London for a couple of days, twiddling my thumbs and not making much progress with the PR plan, when some idiot called me at 6a.m..

"What?" I said, none too politely. There was a pause.

"Darling, daddy's fine," said mummy, "But he's in hospital."

She sounded dreadful.

"Mummy, what's happened?"

I was still a little dazed, but quickly waking up despite the early hour.

Too calmly she explained that that he had had pains in his arm and chest so just to be careful she'd driven him to St. Peter's where Dr. Friedrichs had come to see him. It was a minor heart attack, and he was in for observation, in a quiet little room of his own, until they decided on the best course of action. Mummy quoted medical terms with which I was to become familiar, but which mystified me at the time. When she'd told me everything there was to tell, she just dried up. It was as if she ran out of fuel and rolled to a halt.

"I'll come straight down," I said.

"No darling, no rush," she said idiotically, her upbringing overwhelming her common sense.

We politely squabbled until I told her I'd be there at 10 that morning. After the first awful shock, I found that I wasn't too worried. Perhaps daddy would take it as a warning and cut out some of his worst habits. Dr. Friedrichs had been advising him for years to eat and act sensibly but daddy wouldn't listen. Safely stowed where he could be kept an eye on, hooked up to machines and monitors, the medical staff would be there should the slightest little irregularity occur. I told myself this on the train journey down there.

At the station it was odd not to see daddy's Mercedes or mummy's Range Rover waiting for me; I sat on an uncomfortable bench in the taxi company's office until one of their white Fords turned up. It was unpleasantly fragranced with one of those awful cardboard trees and the stink of cigarette smoke that surrounded the driver. I gave him the hospital's name and he had the decency not to attempt to interest me in whatever opinions he might be harbouring in his nicotine addled brain. I buried my nose in my cashmere sweater's polo neck and comforted myself with the scent of pine logs, spices and Mrs. Newton's kitchen in winter.

A nurse directed me through hundreds of swing doors, to the room where daddy lay in bed, attached to a number of wires, with mummy holding his hand. She looked far worse than he did, not surprising as it turned out that she'd had no sleep and he'd had his longest rest in ages.

"Thank God you're here, darling!" she said, obviously about to burst into tears again, while daddy added, "Loads of fuss, don't know why you bothered, you should be at work."

I was going to explain that I was still having some time off but I decided against adding to their concerns with my little trials. The door opened and a man sidled in and stood quietly until we noticed he was there. I'd barely glanced at him as I passed him sitting in the corridor, but suddenly I gave him a good stare.

"I'll drive you home, shall I, Mrs. Prendergast, if you like?" she said, "Now that Grace is here."

"Oh Kevin, how kind of you," mummy said and as I stared at him some more, he took shape as Kevin from the neighbouring farm, that Kevin. My Kevin. Tall, sandy haired, not especially good looking but resembling an advertisement for the great outdoors. I ought not to have been staring, but I couldn't help noticing that the man was fit.

"You remember Kevin, don't you Grace?" mummy twittered as she assembled her belongings, "from next door, farmer's lad, being so very very helpful. When all this is over, we simply must have you over for dinner, mustn't we? Yes we must."

Kevin and I smiled at each other. Even without make-up I know I'm acceptable, and as it was Kevin, it was probably an advantage to be seen in flats and casuals. A quick glance at his left hand told me that he was as yet unspoken for – he was the kind who would be proud to wear a wedding ring – and as I looked up to his face, I swear that I saw his eyebrows raised and one corner of his mouth turn up in a way which I took to be a positive signal.

Call it the stress of the situation, but when Kevin returned that evening with my mother and offered to drive me home, I took full advantage of the circumstances.

We climbed up into his Land Rover, the smart one, not the field one, and before he'd started the engine, he'd wrinkled his lightly freckled nose, smiled and said, "You smell just like Christmas." By the time he drove me back to St. Peter's the next morning I'd forgotten I'd ever been in love with anyone else.

Daddy knew. I would bet on it. As mummy called out,

"Darling you look awful. Didn't you sleep?" daddy smiled at me.

"Our Kevin's a good chap, isn't he?" he said. "Well built, all that farming work, lots of stamina." I was almost speechless.

"I thought you didn't like him," I said.

"Changed my mind. How about you?"

"Actually, I was always fond of Kevin, but I didn't appreciate his finer points."

"Good on you," said daddy, and we left it at that.

The following week daddy was getting very bored with hospital but he was curiously irritated by the smallest things and clearly not back to normal. His face was pale dishwater colour, and he looked older, smaller and much less powerful. It had diminished him.

His staff, two women and one man, looked after his company, mostly property investments, but as times weren't as busy as in the past, and as they knew the business well enough to take all but the crucial decisions, they got on well enough without him.

Mummy brought him a list of things to approve every day. Nothing that would distress him, just some things to help him feel involved. We'd decided that he was more likely to get upset if he had nothing to do at all and imagined he was being ignored.

His consultant, Mr. Sengupta, decided they would investigate angioplasty, which is to do with sticking something in his artery and inflating it, I think. I stopped listening in case I fainted. His arteries were awfully clogged up, it turned out, so mummy started investing in oats, red wine and balsamic vinegar, everything she'd heard could control cholesterol. When I say investing, she not only stocked up the larder, she went out and bought an Italian goods importer and demanded that Kevin change his planned crop rotation and devote at least one field to oats the following season.

I went into the village with Kevin one night, to the local pub. Mummy thought I deserved a night off to distract myself from the awful times we'd been having. All I'd been doing was hospital visiting, chores, visiting the office and sleeping, she thought. We were back at our local, the place where we all used to meet up during school and college holidays.

I supposed it was our first real date. At the age of ten, we'd both understood that I was his and he was mine, in a pure way that disappears around the age of twelve. When we went to our separate schools, the relationship disintegrated. Decades later, we'd certainly been making up for lost time. I had this dreadfully guilty feeling that Kevin had been holding a candle for me all the while, but I hardly liked to mention it in case it seemed vain.

When we got to the Swan, there was quite a crowd for a Tuesday night. People I saw occasionally - in twos and threes - were assembled into a team, and some I'd not seen for yonks were there too. They all asked kindly about my father; they'd heard that he was getting a little better and someone had thoughtfully organised this amazing, spontaneous gathering to cheer me up. Had I announced that he'd taken a turn for the worse, it would definitely have dampened the jollity.

In one of those totally silent pauses in the chatter, when everyone looks at their watches to see if it's 20 past the hour like the rumours say, but it never is, Johnnie, whose dad is our solicitor, blurted out,

"So are you two seeing each other?" Pins dropped. I just smiled. Kevin put his arm around my shoulder, gripped firmly and said,

"Yes."

Then everyone raised their glasses and said "cheers" and "good for you" and "wonderful news" and I realised that they weren't there simply to cheer me up, they wanted the best bit of local gossip, first hand, that the village had heard all year. Then Johnnie added,

"About bloody time too, Kevin. We thought you'd be single forever."

Miranda, his sister, who was several glasses into the evening, spluttered with laughter and had to put her white wine down while she got herself organised. Kevin had turned pink, quite an exceptional shade.

"It's true," she said, "He's been in love with you since he was seven. I tried, darling, tried and failed, but his heart was only yours."

Then it happened again. I burst into tears. All that time while I had been frittering my life around town, looking for the love of my life and - total cliché - it was the boy next door, even if you did need a horse to visit.

Of course I'd been feeling a little sensitive since the break-up, the surprise at work and poor old daddy's situation, but it struck me all of a sudden that I'd been heartless and hurtful while my wonderful Kevin had been patiently hoping that one day I would see sense. The only problem was that I still hadn't reconciled myself to a phrase that started with "my wonderful" and ended with "Kevin". Oh well, apart from the awfully working class name, he was perfect.

CHAPTER EIGHTEEN - JESSICA

Uncle Mack and my mum were locked up in the front room, well not really locked up, but the door was wasn't wide open as usual, and that doesn't happen, well not much and only if there's something a bit serious going on. I was in the dining room doing my homework, with books all over the table, and she must have noticed that the door wasn't properly shut because I heard her get up, come over and open it. She peered at me like I was a total stranger.

"What are you doing in there?" she said, as if I was trying to burgle the place or something. I sighed noisily, the sign of a stupid question.

"My homework," I said, "like ever."

"Hmmm. Well get on with it."

She shut the door until it clicked so that it wouldn't slide open. I couldn't hear much, and anyway I kept getting distracted by the book I was supposed to be reading, because actually it was quite good. We'd been set a detective story from the 1930s so we could notice the way they used different words from now. Except that I kept forgetting to notice the different words and just kept on reading the story because it was totally interesting.

So when they started to shout I got a bit of a shock. I didn't know whether to go away or to listen harder. I felt a bit sick because I'd never heard them argue before and it reminded me of mum and dad because they used to have rows when he came back from a trip.

I'd forgotten how bad it was. I used to go away and hide upstairs in the attic. But then I decided I wasn't actually going to throw up or faint or anything, so I thought I'd stay and listen.

It was all sort of, "Well if you hadn't gone and ..." and "Well, no-one made you..." and "You're not going to try blaming me for..." and "If you're stupid enough to ..." and "Like I want to follow your brilliant example!" But then unlike mum and dad, just when I was going to go upstairs and shove my fingers in my ears and cry, they started laughing.

"What a pair of idiots we are!" my mum said and then they both laughed and laughed. I wished she'd been like that with my dad. But never mind; I'd got a plan.

Anyway, the next I heard was her saying,

"Yes!" and him saying, "No" and that went on for a while until it seemed like she won.

So the next morning, when I was eating my toast and Marmite, mum said she'd be out that night. She was going out for a drink in London with Uncle Mack because he needed cheering up.

"Shall I make a cheery-up cherry cake for him?" I asked because that was my specialty and I'd been baking loads of them over the last year. Uncle Mack seemed to like them, even when I'd burned one around the edges when I was just learning. Mum laughed like she was mocking me a bit, then she stopped and said,

"Why not? A cake can't do any harm can it, and it might do some good. As long as he doesn't start piling on the pounds and losing his looks. We need to get him married off before he gets set in his ways."

"Mum," I said, not really daring but wanting to know the answer enough to take the risk," what happened to his fiancée?"

"Grace?" she said, "The one who was so stuck up he didn't dare bring her round here? That fiancée?"

"Yes, that one."

"Well, she was being a bit pushy, organising him and so forth and I said to him that he should lay the law down a bit to make sure she knew who was in charge, and it all got a bit out of hand and he called it off. As I understand it, because I wasn't there at the time."

"But couldn't they sort it all out then? If it wasn't that serious?" I asked.

"Ah well, it turns out that there were another couple of complications."

"Like what sort of complications?"

"Well never mind that, but her dad had never liked your uncle anyway. He's the one with all the money, the money that was going to buy the place they were going to live in, and do up the house in Cork."

She looked at me hard and straight in the eyes and sat down opposite me on one of the less wobbly dining chairs.

"It shouldn't all be this complicated, you know," she said, "It should be about love and kindness, but sometimes it's all about money and lies."

She reached over and took my hand, the one without the toast in it, and said, "Promise me Jess, that it'll all be about love and kindness with you and don't say stuff you don't mean to hurt someone's feelings just because you can." Then she got up and went back to filling the washing machine.

"OK," I said.

Mum got back quite early after all, and Uncle Mack was with her. This time they sat in the dining room with me, and talked while I was supposed to be reading. Uncle Mack was going to move into the spare room until he found a little place of his own.

He'd been staying in a hotel while he was visiting London, expecting to be travelling around a bit for his new job. Except that he'd not got the new job, someone else did. Uncle Mack kept going on about how he had practically been promised it, and how he'd been let down and made to look a fool in front of all his colleagues.

From what I could work out, while pretending not to listen at all, this other man didn't seem to have done anything wrong except for getting the job that Uncle Mack thought he should have had, making him look a bit silly.

Mum was really angry and kept going on about the injustice of it all and how the English were always discriminating against the Irish and she was ready to pack her sleeping bag and camp out in the company's front reception until he was restored to his rightful position.

Me, well I couldn't quite make out what the problem was, except that my uncle's feelings were really hurt and he wasn't going to be staying in his cool hotel in the West End any more when he visited for work and because he'd split up with his fiancée, her dad wasn't going to buy them a posh flat. Worse things happen every day at school and you get over them.

"Of course you're welcome to stay here as long as you like," my mum said, then sort of mysteriously she said, "Let's just give her one more try, shall we?" Then they both went completely quiet so I looked up and found them both glancing at me in a very suspicious way, I thought.

"What?" I said.

"Nothing for young ears," my mum said, so that was that.

CHAPTER NINETEEN - DAVID

Grace, it seemed, wasn't going to be back at work for some time, and probably not at all. I had met her father once or twice, but he regarded me as a failure, as I'd settled for managing a family-owned establishment. All the same, I was sorry to hear that he was ill. He is one of those Type A personalities, as I understand they're known, who thrive on stress and business lunches, either of which can do the damage.

So Grace was helping out with his office and it's where she needed to be. I would have liked the chance to spend time with my father too, had he survived his own heart attack.

This left me with a space in my office and too much work for Alice to manage. I had a problem to solve, but this time I knew what it was and where I was going for help. It was wonderful to see Unity again, to sit myself down in the velvet chair and allow it to embrace me, to drink a cup of tea and eat a slice of Bakewell tart. It was interesting to think back over the previous weeks.

Work, I had discovered, was important to me, but my family was at the heart of it all. Perhaps this sounds mundane, and perhaps I am slightly dull after all, but I had identified the things which matter. I felt that I'd renewed a bond with Marianne. I'm not certain of how she'd been feeling about me, and not confident that I would like the answers if I were to choose to ask the questions. Therefore I chose to keep quiet and to accept my new happiness at home.

Once again I found myself holding a china cup, with Unity tucked into the opposite chair.

"Anyway, you look well," she said.

"I'm not doing badly, thanks," I replied then we had exchanged our news, or rather I told her mine.

"I've got a request, "I said, "My assistant, Grace, has decided to take some time away. Personal reasons."

Unity nodded and I recalled that I'd given Grace my appointment the last time I'd seen her. Perhaps they knew each other, but it wasn't my place to enquire. Nor was it relevant.

"So I find myself in need of a new member of staff and I thought about it and wondered if you might be the woman to help me fill the gap."

"Me?" said Unity mildly and took a sip of tea.

"Obviously, I don't expect you to work as my assistant, Unity. Are you being a little disingenuous?"

She smiled.

"What I need is a person who could bring a little creativity to an established organisation, one which needs to be gently but firmly guided into the 21st Century."

"I might know someone at that," she said, which was why the following week I was sitting in our conference room with a young woman whose presence lit up its fusty interior with a delightful new spirit. Phoebe didn't question why she'd been invited to visit, but was pleasantly cheered when I told her. Her underestimation of her own potential had a genuine charm.

Her department was "restructuring" she told me, so I took advantage and called her manager about releasing her early, and negotiated a two week notice period, only one of which she was obliged to work. This was with her express permission of course. She was terrifically pleased with the result, as we all were. I started to worry. When things run this smoothly they can speed up and crash. Then I decided it would probably be fine.

I had a feeling I'd heard of her former employer so I asked Alice.

"Oh yes," she said, "That's where Grace's ex-fiancé worked,

"Perhaps they know each other."

"Perhaps best not to ask." She grinned at me in a most un-Alice-like way, so I nodded and smiled back, puzzled but suspecting that she was right.

"Do you think it likely that Grace would ever want to return?" I asked, adding, "I don't wish to go behind her back, as it were, but I wondered if you might be party to information which would suggest a decision one way or the other. And I certainly don't require the details. It's just that I had the impression she thought she might be hurting my feelings if she told me I would never see her again."

"That sounds like Grace, "Alice said, smiling again. "No, I don't think she'll be back; I think she'll marry her childhood sweetheart and I think she didn't want to tell you because…" and she looked me right in the eyes, raised her eyebrows and said, "…because she was under the impression that you were secretly in love with her."

"No!" I said, "She wasn't! Surely not. Was she? How extraordinary! What on earth could have given her that idea? In love with her? How extraordinary! Where on earth did she get that idea?"

Alice was clearly amused by my surprise, but interrupted my inane gabbling.

"Don't worry about it," she said, "Grace is like that. She thinks everyone's in love with her. Or they ought to be."

"Was it when I took her out to lunch? After her engagement ended. Was that it? I was just trying to be considerate."

"That merely confirmed her suspicions. But really, don't worry about it. You don't know what drives our Grace. She could never be alone for long. She was looking for a replacement and she thought you had potential."

"Potential? But I'm married."

"I think that was the biggest obstacle, but a man who's been married once has a track record. Men who stay single into their thirties are often a complete mistake; they like it too much. Actually, I don't think you were from a good enough family, but you were on her radar."

"Extraordinary," I said, and that was the end of it. "So we're looking forward to working with Phoebe, then?"

"What a little sweetheart," said Alice, "I think she'll do wonders for us. And she's got a boyfriend, so you're safe."

Alice and I had never had a similar conversation, and I found myself looking forward to getting to know her better, strictly as a colleague of course.

111

CHAPTER TWENTY - JESSICA

I dropped in to see Giorgio and Alessandro again on the way to Unity's. This time I wasn't that early so I told them I'd call back for a hot chocolate on the way home. I don't think Unity normally does Saturdays but she does it for me because of school and homework. Oh my god it was freezing outside.

It had stopped being autumn overnight and turned into the Arctic or something. It was so nice to get inside the big black door. I'd nearly fallen flat on the cobbles because it was frosty in the shade where the sun hadn't reached. It was way too cold for a smoothie.

We got all settled into our chairs by a real fire. We can't have fires at home because my mum says the boys would burn the house down and I suppose that's reasonable, because they probably would. Unity did me a hot blackcurrant and gave me a fairy cake with pink icing and silver sugar balls. I wondered how come she wasn't fat, but maybe she gives them all away.

I told her how my plan was coming along. I was thinking that we could have a day out with dad and my brothers and that maybe I could get my mum to come too. We would go to the Science Museum in time to see the beam engine running because our dad is totally obsessed with that, and then we would all go and have tea and cakes at the Hungarian café near the station.

I said that I'd got my mum to say yes, "in principle" she said, because my brothers really needed to see us all together as a family. I told my dad the same thing too and I think he'll do it, because I piled it on a bit about how important it is for my brothers.

"I admire your ingenuity," she said, "But don't expect too much to come from it. Aim for a nice day out, not for a whole change in the way your family lives. That way you'll stand a good chance of having a nice day out. The best way to ruin it would be to have an ulterior motive."

"Yes," I said, "A nice day out would be good. And Unity do you mind if I ask you something stupid?"

"Ask away."

"When people talk about ulterior motives, I sort of know what it means but not really. So what it is exactly?"

"Ah, yes," she said, "Lots of people use phrases they've picked up without checking first, so it's a good idea to ask. So it's not stupid, it's intelligent. It's when you say you're doing something for one reason, but you have a secret extra reason that the others concerned don't know about."

"And is it always wrong?"

She thought for a bit.

"Not always," she said, "If you buy your friend a bicycle for her birthday, it's because you want to give her a present, but your ulterior motive might be that you think she's a bit unfit and could do with some exercise. So if she sells the bike and uses the money to pay for taxis, then you've only yourself to blame."

"I think I get it," I said, "I shouldn't kid myself that it's for any reason except that I'd like us all to have a nice day out. And I shouldn't make out that it's for my brothers when really it's me who wants it to happen. And I really really really shouldn't be doing it in the hope that if I can get them all in the same place that my mum will forgive my dad and that he'll come back to live at our house. Because that's really what I want."

She smiled a bit sort of sadly, "Yup, that's it."

"Instead of making up all these stories in my head about the future, about when my dad comes home again, and them never fighting any more, I'll just make up stories about having a nice day out at the Science Museum."

"Set a realistic target."

"No shouting for four hours?"

"Brilliant. What you've done, organising a trip out to get your family together for the afternoon, that's wonderful, do you know that? Ulterior motive or not, it's a lovely thing to do. So let's hope that your mum and dad can behave themselves as responsibly as you do, and make it a good day out."

"But secretly can I wish for it all to be OK again?"

"No-one can stop you doing that, Jessica, and as long as you don't wish your life away spending time on things which you can't control, you're allowed a bit of it. But if you find yourself feeling sad because it's not the way you want it, you have to stop and think about something useful. If you find you've sat there for a while inventing your perfect family, get up and finish your homework, or go for a walk and visit your friends. It's not good to use up all your emotional energy on fantasies, but you're definitely allowed to devote it to good, workable ideas."

"Like making cakes?"

"Perfect."

"Is that why you make so many cakes?"

Unity shrieked with laughter. I wasn't expecting that.

"You're probably right," she said.

Giorgio was having a quiet day. He told me that they didn't used to open at all on a Saturday but then people started to come by at the weekend too, and it turned into a different sort of an atmosphere, with less of a rush like on work days, and more of a calm, relaxing read the papers sort of "vibe" he said. So while Alessandro made the coffees for people and warmed up their croissants, and did their cream cheese and smoked salmon bagels, Giorgio sat down at my table and interrogated me while I had my hot chocolate with a splash of caramel syrup. He asked me how old I was before he told me that he and Alessandro were gay. And I said it was OK because I already knew some people who were gay. He said that he'd come over from Italy because it was more difficult where he came from to be both gay and normal. You could be gay, he said, in his town, but only if you were going to be singled out as the gay one, because they liked to think they were tolerant, but they weren't that tolerant. You'd get invited to dinner by people who wanted to show that they had a gay friend, not because they were interested in your opinions on football or films or anything at all. He could have gone to Milan and blended in, he said, but he fancied London. When he arrived he met Alessandro, who'd had the same idea. I thought that was very interesting because I'd not thought about it before and I like to think about things I'd never thought about before. It was amazing coming to Unity's and seeing Giorgio on the way home. It was my whole secret world. I wondered if I'd ever see the woman on the bus again, because since the day with the invitation, I don't think we'd ever caught the same one.

The day we went out it was sunny, which was good because we could walk without rushing and the boys didn't complain about getting wet feet. They always splash in the puddles; they really don't think it through. We went to the museum and the boys looked at the space things and I liked the household bit the best where you could look back at the kind of inventions that your gran used to have. Then we had our tea and cakes and I thought about Unity and how I wasn't to listen to my ulterior motives, but everything seemed to be going OK and I couldn't help hoping just a little bit. My mum and dad had been doing a funny sort of dance where they made sure that they didn't have to stand close enough to each other to have to talk. When we all sat down they couldn't really avoid it. I just stayed quiet and kept my fingers crossed that they wouldn't argue in public. Apart from a few goes from my mother, which my dad managed to ignore, I felt like it went quite well.

My dad said he'd buy us dinner so we all went back to Pizza on the Green in Ealing. It was OK too but I was a bit too nervous to eat much. I said it was because I'd already had cake because it was true anyway.

"You're a bit thin," my dad said.

"She's not anorexic. She eats loads at home," my mum said a bit snappishly so I stepped in and reminded them that it had been a really big cake only a couple of hours before and that no-one expects girls to wolf it all down like growing boys. Chris and Jeff ate the rest of my pizza so it wasn't as if it was wasted. There was a bit of a pause at the end of the meal and I was sort of wishing my mum would say,

"It's been such a wonderful day out, John. Why don't you come home to us and we'll start all over again and do it right this time?" but then I remembered what Unity said. I put my elbow on the table and rested my chin on my hand so I could have a good sniff of my seaside scent and I said,

"Well this has been very nice. Maybe one day we can do it again." I was hoping for a bit of back-up from my brothers but they just looked blank like a pair of idiots and Chris said,

"I've got just a bit of maths homework I forgot about so if we're all finished up here I could do with getting back."

"Right then," said dad.

"You were supposed to finish it before we went out," said mum, and sighed.

"Yeah well anyway, mum," said Chris, "Can dad come back and help me with the maths?" and then I nearly froze with excitement or something because he'd not been back to the house since the day he left and she said, "Yes, of course, if he's got the time. You can't just go asking favours like that at short notice."

"I can help," dad said, "No particular hurry to get home." I could see that mum nearly joined in with the usual, something like, "No, not now the bitch has run off and left you all alone," like she would if she thought we couldn't hear so I stared and her and somehow got her attention, and she stopped. She didn't even start. So I smiled.

At the house, dad commented on the changes; there wasn't a lot, just some old pictures that mum had put up, and a new colour of paint in the hall where the boys had scraped their bicycles along the walls until mum said it wasn't fit for polite people to visit. Then he said he'd got new phones for us. They were brilliant! We were sitting around the dining table playing with them, and the boys were being really irritating testing ringtones until mum and dad couldn't stand it any longer and mum told them to go to their rooms.

Dad went and helped with Chris's maths which only took about 20 minutes after all that fuss, but then homework always went faster with dad about. Then we were all hanging around the dining room again testing out apps to see what they did because this wasn't just a little upgrade for us, this was like going to live on another planet. I'd just got on to voice record and put it down at the end of the table to see what it would pick up and Jeff said, "So dad, will you come over every week and help with homework?" and it all went quiet. Mum gave him a freezing stare and dad just looked down at the table top, all sombre of a sudden like when you hear that someone's gran's died and you don't know what you're supposed to say to them.

"Kids. Out." said mum and as I went towards the end of the table to get my phone she said, "I said "out", now. You can do without your posh new phone for five minutes, can't you?" and I wanted to say, "But mum it might be recording everything you say, probably," but I couldn't which is why later I heard this (missing out the pauses and the humms and ahhs):

Mum (coldly): Well that's never going to happen.

Dad (sounding tired): Don't start, Josie.

Mum: You might recall that it wasn't me that started it.

Dad (big sigh): Josie, I know why I'm here. It's because Jess, bless her little heart, believes that one day, if you can only forgive me for my unforgivable behaviour, I'll come back in a flash and we can be one big happily family again.

Mum: As if!

Dad: Just knock it off, Josie. Finally and forever will you give up this ridiculous posturing? I know about the man down the road, him with the dog. I'd known for ages before my daft little dalliance. I was tired of it all, you and your behaviour, taking advantage of me. You'd long since lost interest; what did you expect?...

(Mum kept trying to butt in but he told her to be quiet and listen a few times.)

... So when you wanted a divorce, I gave you what you asked for; the house, the kids, maintenance, and your fine reputation as a wronged wife firmly intact. But remember this, I could have countersued. I could have divorced you long since, I could have left you with nothing much at all. But I didn't. I'm happy now with my little flat.

Mum (interrupting successfully): With your 23-year-old floozy to keep it nice and tidy for you!

Dad: I live alone, Josephine. That's all over. It was some kind of passing phase, a catalyst to force me to make a decision and get out of that dreadful situation.

Mum (sarcastically): Our marriage you mean.

Dad: (pause)

Mum: You left your children as the result of a pathetic affair.

Dad: Josie, I left because you don't like me. You were nasty, unkind, unfaithful and you seemed to take pleasure in deliberately making me unhappy. Have you managed to forget that?

Mum: Apparently. You left. That's what I remember.

Dad: (Sigh) Do you know why I'm here, going through this again? Because Jessica needs some stability, some sign that it's not all going to be about bitterness and anger, and I'm willing to have a go at being friends. That's all. You've convinced the poor child that if you can summon the kindness to ask, that I'd drop everything and come running back. No! Be quiet and listen. Do you not get that I'd had enough of it?

Look Josie, You can decide to take your half of the responsibility for this; you can accept that I could have behaved far worse towards you. If I'd felt like it, you could be the one alone in a little flat with limited access to your own children. The way you behaved towards me and towards them? I could have damaged you. Now all you do is this point-scoring, moaning about how unfortunate you are, whinging and carping on all the time, making yourself miserable and boring the hell out of the few friends you've got left.

Now look. You don't need this huge house. You'd get by with three, maybe four bedrooms. A nice terrace with the loft done. Sell it, move down the road and keep the profit. Get yourself a part-time job, woman. And bear in mind that if you keep on shoving me, I could consider getting the lawyers back and renegotiating. Josie, I have tried to be tolerant and reasonable. But nothing on earth would get me back under the same roof as you and your two-faced, self-righteous ways. I'm not sitting here waiting for you to forgive me, Josie, and I'm not coming back. As the kids say, deal with it.

Mum: (Nothing, but I think I heard a bit of a gasp.)

Dad: So I'll leave you to think it through and I'll say good bye to the kids. It breaks my heart to leave them, just so you know. I'll do this again, if you like, when you invite me. In the meantime perhaps you'd like to give some thought to what really happened to make our marriage fall apart.

Then there was the noise of chairs moving and general scuffling about and that was it.

So that was a bit of a surprise.

CHAPTER TWENTY-ONE – GRACE

I'd forgotten about the estate agent. When my phone rang, showing an unidentified central London number, I had no idea who was calling.

"Hi Grace? It's Tristan here, from Hayes, Nobbs and Mickelthwaite," said a smart voice and I thought for a moment and said, "Oh yes," and hoped he would give me a clue so I wouldn't have to make an idiot of myself.

"It's just that we would like to arrange a viewing."

"Oh right." Got it!

"Yes, a girl, first time buyer, and she's expressed an interest in a viewing at your earliest convenience. Unusual at this time of year as they often wait until spring, but it seems as though mummy and daddy would like to get her something nice for Christmas. Not that we'd expect to complete by then, oh no no no, but it would be nice to exchange, wouldn't it?"

"Yes lovely," I said, catching up swiftly. Sitting in mummy's generously proportioned kitchen – everything mummy owns is generously proportioned – with a cup of chamomile tea, my London flat seemed like another world. It was ages since I'd been there.

"So would it be OK for me to do the viewing myself, or would you prefer to be present?"

So I hot-footed it back to London that lunchtime to smarten it up a little. Obviously I kept the place tidy but there could always be the odd pair of knickers hanging about on the radiator. It was strange to be home. I'd forgotten the place in the rush of other things; family emergencies and tremendously exciting new relationships do rather wear out ones resources. And it's only when one sits on ones sofa with a week's post that one realises how exhausted one is.

When I woke up, it was already four and almost dark. I whooshed round with the vacuum cleaner and sorted out the bills from the bumph, which is the reason that I came to be holding a handwritten envelope from someone whose writing I didn't recognise. One recognises ones aunts' hands and who else goes to the trouble these days?

It was written in blue ballpoint and it went like this:

I am writing on behalf of my brother, Cormac, who doesn't know anything about this. He has been devastated by the end of your engagement. I don't know the exact circumstances as he cannot bring himself to discuss it, and he will not contact you directly for fear of rejection.

I ask just one thing. Would you please let me know if you have it in your heart to consider a reconciliation? Either way, please would you send me a short note in response, That way, we, his loving family, could hope to put an end his torment one way or another.

Sincerely yours,

Josephine Tuttle.

The estate agent was due at seven. I had less than two hours to make the place perfect, and sort myself out emotionally after that little bombshell added to everything else. Did I still want to sell the flat even? Was it wiser to keep a place on in London, despite starting a lovely new life in the country? One needs a bolt-hole, doesn't one? My parents' house being just a smidgen too close to the centre of the action, so to speak.

But, about the letter. Excuse me, but what on earth? Who was this Josephine Tuttle, queen of drama? His sister? The one who was so keen to split us up in the first place? End his torment? Euthanasia would be my answer to that. Did I ever want to speak to Cormac again? Let alone give him another chance. No, no and no. Whatever the next question was, the answer was already no.

I got up and gave the flat the final once-over. As I ducked down to check under the bed, I found one of his spotted socks! Although my natural inclination was to put it in the washing and iron it, I threw it in the kitchen bin. My decision was made. I would sell. I did not wish to hold on to the site of my failed engagement. I would sell, then buy something different!

The letter; what to do? I replied. I wrote that I was sorry but that I was no longer interested in a reconciliation, that I appreciated her kind thoughts and that she had her brother's best interests at heart but that I no longer felt the same way about him and that it would be better for him to move on. Then I put it in an envelope, stamped and addressed it, put on my hat, coat and gloves and walked straight to the post box and shoved it right in there, making sure it wasn't extractable, and wiped that particular slate clean. Done. Then I went home, unwrapped myself, put on the coffee and waited for the doorbell to ring.

The flat is sold! (Subject to contract and all the usual legal fuss and bother.) Frankly, I don't think we need to worry save for an Act of God. Lovely people, Italians, who want a place that's reasonably handy for the Royal College of Music where Oriana will be studying flute. I'd say she had a charmed life, but at the moment so do I, so I don't begrudge her. They'd called the next day, offered the asking price and suggested that I might take it off the market. Of course I would! I'm not greedy; I'm delighted that it's working out so well for all of us. Let's not rock the boat by being silly about money.

One slightly odd thing happened a couple of days after the viewing. I was going to meet mummy in town for a day at the shops. The poor darling had had no fun in recent weeks so we thought we'd go for a tasty snack and treat ourselves to a bottle of perfume at the lovely shop in Elizabeth Street, then get the train back to the country together. A woman on my bus also got off at Victoria. Then she followed me into the café where mummy was waiting and sat alone glowering at us. I say followed, but it's perfectly possible that she just happened to be going to the same place and coincidentally travelled on the same bus. You would, if that's where you were heading, and stranger things happen. One can take that particular bus as it doesn't pass through anywhere dreadful. I'm not saying that she was actually stalking me, as such.

I went to the ladies' and she came walking through the door as I was washing my hands. I was almost certain that she was poised to say something to me. As I took my little blue bottle from my bag and applied my special, "By the log fire in the farmhouse kitchen" scent she started hard at it, then turned and shut herself in a cubicle. We left, headed over the street to get mummy a nice bottle of fragrance for herself, and that was the end of it. She's probably just one of those wombats who doesn't like other people's perfume. Or I was imagining things.

CHAPTER TWENTY-TWO - THE NEWS

24 Hour Rolling News
Sunday Morning 9a.m.

Studio, with Mike Bayley. Dramatic music.

Mike: A suspected terrorist attack caused central London to be totally evacuated in the early hours of this morning, when a gas cloud was released at approximately 3a.m.. Police have now allowed traffic and pedestrians back into the area surrounding the epicentre of the strike, having ensured that it's now safe.

Late night party-goers and shift workers remained calm as they were shepherded by the emergency services from the Bloomsbury area near London's busy Covent Garden, after what was originally thought to be a chemical attack. Police scientists are investigating the gas cloud and its source.

Earlier today Chief Superintendent Henrietta Overdean of the Metropolitan Police issued this statement:

Cut to Press Conference:

Chief Superintendent Henrietta Overdean:

This morning at approximately three fifteen, the police were alerted to an unusual concentration of gaseous substances in the Bloomsbury area of central London. The source of the gas has been traced and police are investigating the facilities contained there. The owners are being questioned.

Several passers-by were taken to hospital with suspected poisoning, and are being kept under observation until the source of their illness is determined.

Cut to Studio:

Mike: Chief Superintendent Henrietta Overdean speaking earlier. We can now go to Sara Sharman who is in central London.

Sara, it appears that poisoned gas has affected several people.

Cut to Bloomsbury (where Sara Sharman looks very cold indeed):

Sara: Yes Mike. Several people were taken by ambulance to St. Francis' Hospital last night but unofficially one A&E doctor told me that it was business as usual for a Saturday night, so Mike, we are still uncertain as to the cause of the poisoning. I'm led to understand that it could have been one too many cocktails in central London's busy clubs.

But for the moment, police aren't ruling out a dangerous attempt to poison all of central London and bring the city to its knees. It's possible that this was a dry run to test dispersion techniques for a more serious attack and emergency services are not dismissing any of the options.

Mike: And about the building's owners. We believe that the police are questioning them now.

Sara: It's understood that the building houses a secret chemical laboratory, but whether or not the gas was released on purpose or by accident has yet to be ascertained. Police have not yet released any information on the two people they are questioning.

Cut to Studio:

Mike: More on the Bloomsbury dirty bomb later. Now, the football.

CHAPTER TWENTY-THREE - JESSICA

Anyway, I was still getting over all that stuff about my mum and dad. It was funny to know the background to it. I mean not funny, just weird. It made me cry a bit because I felt really sorry for my dad because he'd been unhappy and we never knew about that. He was supposed to have been mean and selfish. And my mum and the man from the park with the dog? Eeeuw! I didn't want to think about that but it kept on turning up in my head. They really did it, probably, but where? Our house, his house? Did they tie up the dog and snog on a park bench. I just had to not think about it because it was putting me off.

So anyway, I asked if I could spend the next weekend at dad's. Mum had encouraged us to stay away from his flat saying that he wouldn't want us there with his "fancy woman" but I decided she was probably wrong about that and I wanted to make up for some of the times I'd stayed here when it was supposed to be his turn. Usually that would have started an argument so when she said yes straight off it was a surprise.

"Take your brothers as well," she said. "Your uncle's going to Ireland so I'll have a nice quiet weekend on my own." I expect she was planning to get the man with the dog round to our house. I decided to look for evidence of dog hair when I got back again.

So off we went on Friday night with our backpacks full of homework and spare clothes. Dad's flat was really nice and warm and he'd cooked us lasagne. On Saturday morning he made us clean the place to earn some pocket money and he set us a competition for who could get our bits of the flat the most spotless. Then he did us omelettes and he made us do our homework and we went to a concert at the Albert Hall which was mostly good but a little bit too long. One of his colleagues was singing in the choir and it turned out to be a man, not a new girlfriend or anything like that.

So on Sunday morning when the news came on I went white and dad thought I was going to faint. All those policemen and fire engines and reporters on the news; I went all horrible inside thinking about it. Dad looked really worried and wanted to know what was wrong with me, and I nearly cried a bit and my brothers were staring so we went into my room and I told him the whole story about Unity and he was dead worried and a bit cross because he said it could have been a trap and I should never have done a stupid thing like that and I could have been kidnapped. So I told him that I'd had coffee with Giorgio first – then I had to explain about Giorgio not being interested in teenage girls like not at all – and he said it was fine, and we ended up saying that we would all go to see Giorgio and possibly Unity and Carl, so dad could meet my friends and then he'd take the boys to the British Museum to see all the Roman stuff they go bonkers about.

My dad said it was obvious that it was all a lot of fuss about nothing because if there was a real threat the press wouldn't have been there so I didn't have to worry.

Then I calmed down, then he calmed down and said he was really sorry that he hadn't taken enough notice of me and that I'd had no-one to talk to and that he hoped I would pick up the phone for a chat in future if I needed to, And I said yes, I would but I wasn't really sure I meant it because he's, like, my dad? And they don't really know that much about life. Not like Unity.

So we got off at Covent Garden station because my dad said we could walk from there and I was really surprised, but he was right and Unity's was really close to shops and things. As we got closer, Chris and Jeff got all interested in the fire engines and said that some of the cars were Anti-Terrorist Squad and that you could tell, but the people in them didn't look like police, they looked like actors, so I wasn't sure. And we got to Giorgio's where he came out and shook me by the hand with both of his and said, "Come in, come in, a caramel chocolate, yes? And for the boys, the same with marshmallows, and for Jessica's father a nice mocchachino on such a cold day, yes?"

So my dad was all prepared for some serious words and he just got befriended like everyone is. We were drinking our drinks and using the mugs to keep our hands warm, and sort of whispering about what on earth was going on, because we'd not really worked it out. It was pretty noisy in the café because everyone was talking into their mobile phones. So then Giorgio came and sat at our table and looked around to see who was listening. He explained in a kind of whisper what had happened. Someone had broken in, smashed up Unity's place and then because of the smell, people thought it was a chemical weapons attack, although they must have been idiots because it was obviously perfume. Then Unity got a phone call in the middle of the night practically, and had to come over. They gave her a really hard time until the scientists realised it was all scent. And by that time it was the coffee time just about so she and Carl went to Giorgio's.

And then he picked up our coats off our chairs and sort of announced, "You know, it's getting really busy in here, you can sit in the annexe," and looked at me and made the sign for lips sealed before I could say "what annexe?" I picked up my bag and my hot chocolate and set off after him. Dad budged Chris and Jeff out of their places and came too. Just then there was a shout in the street, and everyone else in the café picked up their stuff and shoved their way out of there.

"Alessandro, get the place filled up with the emergency services, would you my darling? And don't let the media back in. It's not safe."

We walked through a swing door, down a hall and into a bright, sunny living room which was really warm and nice, and huge. Unity and Carl were sitting by the fire looking a bit upset, I thought.

"Jessica. What are you doing here?" she got up and gave me a big hug.

"We saw it on the news and we thought we'd better come over." I said. "This is my dad, John, and my brothers, Chris and Jeff. And dad this is Unity and Carl." Everyone said hello and shuffled around a bit.

"My dad's going to the museum with the boys, and I had to tell him all about what we've been doing and now's not the best time but he did get a bit cross about me not going off with strangers, didn't you dad?" Dad looked embarrassed.

"You didn't know?" Unity asked my dad.

"Was I supposed to tell him?" I asked.

"Oh Jessica!" they both said at once, and then I was nearly crying because it was all my fault now and it had been a really bad day and it wasn't even lunch time yet. So my dad took over.

"Unity, I'm so pleased to meet you. I'm sorry it's under such dreadful circumstances."

"You calling my circumstances dreadful?" said Giorgio, waving his arms around at all the treasures in the room, and then he shut up quickly and guided my brothers to the other end of the room to show them some books or something.

"I'd no idea," Unity said.

"That's not important now," said my dad like he was completely in charge. "You've done a good thing for my daughter, and it's helped me to realise that I need to put in a bit more effort with my own kids. I'm just fortunate that while I was neglecting her, she found someone like you."

Unity managed a bit of a smile but not like normal.

"Anyway," said my dad, "Today's not about us, so we'll be off to the museum now. Come on lads."

"Can I stay and help, dad? If I'm not in the way," I asked. Giorgio had drifted back.

"Can you wash up, Jessica?" he said.

And so I got to stay.

The next people who got there were called Phoebe and Chandra who were really nice too. They brought Chandra's cousin and his wife, who wasn't really his wife, because she had a girlfriend who was there too with her husband who was Chandra's cousin's partner, which was all really amazing because it was like being in a soap.

CHAPTER TWENTY-FOUR - DAVID

On the 24 hour news programme, a reporter was stringing out the story to last for the allocated number of minutes before the newsreader in the studio moved on to the next subject, trying to make it sound more exciting than it obviously was. Marianne and I watched on a small television in the kitchen which the girls had switched on to see a noisy Japanese cartoon, then left as they wandered away to their rooms to do something more intellectually engaging. I hoped. They tell me to be environmentally conscious, but they are very easily distracted. Watching the report, I didn't want to say anything but Marianne had noticed.

"It looks awfully close to Unity's place, doesn't it?" she said.

"A bit, yes." I said. "Have they mentioned the exact spot?"

"They just said Bloomsbury."

"Right."

"Do you think we ought to go over there to see if she's OK?"

"What could we do?" I said, "If she's fine, she's fine, and if she's not....? And what if it's actually dangerous?"

"Let's go anyway," Marianne said, placing her knife on her plate as she made her mind up. "Because, look at it this way, if it was really a terrorist attack, someone would have been killed and the reporters would be allowed nowhere near the place, and they'd have a proper story, and the buses wouldn't be going by. Look."

We watched the screen as a red double-decker went past the reporter, who was repeating herself, again.

"They're just making a fuss to keep their faces on screen and stop us turning over to something more interesting," said my cynical, practical wife. "Everyone loves a bit of drama on a Sunday morning."

"But what if it's really dangerous?" I said again.

"The police will send us home, my darling."

Sadie and Clara were due to go out with friends, so we got them bundled up into their down jackets and protective headgear in time to join a bicycle trip to Chiswick House. It was to be led by one of the mothers I'd probably met at a school parents' evening. You worry about it, but you can't keep them indoors all the time.

We checked online that the tubes were running, wrapped ourselves up warm too and took a brisk walk to the station. Half an hour and a glut of Christmas shopping tourists later, we emerged from Holborn's claustrophobia-inducing depths to a crisp winter noon that smelled of coffee and cakes, to find a fleet of fire engines parked all down Kingsway. One huge red van had smart gold lettering naming it the "Incident Control Vehicle" and another said, "Scientific Support Unit."

There were men with gas masks and goggles dangling round their necks and one with his fluorescent waistcoat labelled HAZMAT OFFICER. I guessed at Hazardous Materials. Why not write it out properly? I was beginning to sound like my father, even to myself. None of them seemed worried about being there, despite the news channels' undignified excitement about chemical warfare and dirty bombs.

We walked towards Bloomsbury Mews and passed fire engines whose badges indicated that they'd come from throughout central London: Clerkenwell, Paddington, Euston, Soho, maybe more. Police cars were parked with their blue lights flashing, but nothing appeared to be happening.

Wherever one finds a crowd of firemen, I have observed that an equally sized crowd of flirtatious women will gather. Where did they come from on a Sunday morning? Marianne ascertained that they were the leftovers from a long weekend, out for a final stroll before taking the train back to Leeds. She wandered off and started chatting with one of the older firemen, a disconcertingly handsome fellow with cropped grey hair and handsome bone structure. I strolled on several yards so she could carry out her investigations unimpeded by a visible husband.

She caught up with me to report that there had been a chemical spillage up the road, all safe now and nothing to worry about. On enquiring if it could have been a terrorist attack, the film star fireman reassured her that if there was even a whiff of the serious stuff about, the whole area would be blocked off and they'd be parked three miles down the road while the anti-terrorist lads took over. On sympathising that they had to stand around with nothing to do, the fireman had remarked that it was better than sitting around at base the nothing to do. Apparently, there were 25 fire appliances in the vicinity. Quite an outing.

Heading towards the mews, we saw more appliances (the technical term, Marianne told me, not "engines"), yet more police flashing lights and people standing around. We could smell fragrant flowers growing somewhere close by.

"There's Giorgio," said Marianne, as a dark haired chap scuttled out of a café balancing a large tray of hot drinks which he distributed to the waiting firemen.

"He'll be loving all that," she said, smiling.

"How do you know Giorgio?" I asked, wondering about my wife's secret life.

"Everyone goes into his café if they're a bit early for their appointment at 25, or afterwards for a thinking break before going back to their normal lives. He and Alessandro are complete darlings; they make all their money in the morning rush, then for the rest of the day they run a kind of social club for people at a loose end. They do Unity and Carl a special Ethiopian blend."

I raised my eyebrows, having realised that I'd done exactly that on the day of my first appointment. I ought to talk to my wife more, I told myself, as I could learn all manner of things I'd no idea I needed to know. We were wordlessly approaching the hub, and Marianne took my gloved hand in hers when we saw that the mews was guarded by police and had blue and white striped tape flimsily barring the entrance. We stopped walking and stared.

"The air," said Marianne. "Smell it." The whole of London seemed to be scented with a delightful mixture of flowers, cakes, chocolate and spices which had got stronger as we got closer. "It's coming from Unity's place."

Perhaps we ought to have felt more concerned, but the scent of florist, patisserie and confectioner all blended together was so pacifying that it took the edge off it.

"I'm sure everything's going to be fine." I knew this sounded idiotic as I said it, but I felt as though I'd swallowed a magical happy pill. Near the mews entrance, the scent was so all encompassing that I wanted to walk closer and breathe more deeply.

"Sorry sir, you can't go past the barrier. Crime scene," said one of the young officers posted at the corner. In the background there was a shuffle among the collection of media people who were huddled together for warmth. Fluffy things on long sticks crept towards us hovering above our hats, and notebooks flipped open.

"What's happened?" Marianne asked. "Is it number 25?"

"We're not at liberty to say, madam," said the older of the two policemen. Auto-focus cameras beeped and shutters clicked.

"Are you Unity's friends?" called a woman, approaching us. I stepped in, wary of what I was saying and to whom.

"It's Unity's place, is it? I said.

"Have you come to meet her? Name?"

"Where is she? What does she make in the lab?"

"Does she have links to extremist groups?"

I was too calm to argue, or even be outraged by their questions, so I took Marianne's hand again and tried to move away but we'd been circled.

"Describe the laboratory, will you?"

"Excuse me! Over here! Is that a Paul Smith coat you're wearing?"

Some flashes went off.

"This is awful," Marianne whispered. "How was that relevant anyway? Is this the news or the fashion police?"

"What's awful?" shouted a man at the back.

"Excuse us," I said and pushed as politely as I could manage through the crowd until we popped out into a clear space. As we turned away a couple of men, one very tall, athletic and black, one less tall, less athletic and white - plain clothes police I would imagine - came out of number 25 and everyone's attention was drawn away from us.

"There's nothing we can do," Marianne said.

"No."

"So let's go and see Giorgio and Alessandro and get a coffee."

When we got inside, Giorgio had fulfilled all the firemen's current needs and come in to wash up and restock his counter.

"Marianne," he called as we came in, skirting around the busy tables to take her by both hands and kissing her on both cheeks. "And this is your handsome husband? I hope so!"

"Giorgio, this is David, my handsome husband." He gave me a sharp look down and up and stared me in the eyes."

"A cup of tea, I think," he said. "I'll give you a house special with cardamom, cinnamon, clove and hot milk. For the shock," and shot back to his venerable coffee machine where he filled, fitted, clattered, pulled and pushed items of coffee paraphernalia to produce what he'd decided we needed. He raised an eyebrow to Alessandro, who was tidying tables and allocating them to members of the emergency services who were half hoping for something exciting to do and half relieved that nothing terrible had happened. Anyone who looked the slightest bit like a reporter was gently blocked at the door. I did feel a little sorry for them, stuck in the cold with a job to do, but there were other cafés that would appreciate their business.

"Come through," said Giorgio, carrying our cups with him through to the kitchen. Opening an old wooden door at the back with his elbow, he led us along a passageway into a large, high sitting room, warmed with an open fire. The sun shone through huge arched windows into one of the most spectacular Georgian rooms I've ever been in, if you don't count private clubs and National Trust houses. It was furnished with a collection of fine antiques and tasteful modern stuff, rather like Unity's place but on a much grander scale. At one end, a group of people sat around the dining table drinking coffee, and in the settees by the fire were Unity, Carl and a girl I thought I recognised.

"Hello Mrs Cavendish. Hello Mr Cavendish."

"Hello Jessica," Marianne said. "David, you remember Jessica, Josie's daughter."

"Yes of course, but you're taller," I said, which was unnecessary but true.

"My dad and Chris and Jeff were here, but they've gone to the British Museum," she said, looking me right in the eye and smiling. "Are you Unity's friends too?"

"Yes, we are." I said.

"Hello David," said Phoebe from the other side of the room where I hadn't noticed her sitting amongst the group. "Let's get organised, then I'll introduce you properly. Come and sit down. You must be Marianne. I'm Phoebe, David's new assistant. I replaced Grace when her dad had a heart attack."

"Chandra," said Chandra politely standing up and putting out his hand.

"Like the moon," said Marianne, accepting it.

"Exactly," chorused the committee at the dining room table, smiling.

"This is the emergency cabinet," Phoebe announced. "We're trying to work out who could do such a horrible thing to Unity."

CHAPTER TWENTY-FIVE - DAVID

"What actually happened?" Marianne asked no one in particular, glancing at Unity. Carl answered.

"Someone broke in early this morning. It's a big old door but it's got a simple lock, so we're told. Someone picked it, went upstairs and smashed up the scent store then sprayed the words 'You've ruined my life' along the downstairs corridor. Apparently most of London could smell it. We've no idea who did it. As far as we know, Unity has no sworn enemies and we can't think of anyone with a motive, as the detectives say. The person wore gloves and the police haven't found any other clues yet.

"But that's awful," said Marianne, "Why would anyone? Surely all you do is help people sort their lives out?"

"Yes well...," said Carl, "There are a few who've had their lives indirectly sorted out for them along the way. Fallout, so to speak. Say if one person's problem was another person. That happens."

"I hate this," Unity said quietly. "There's someone out there who despises me enough to smash my life's work to bits and we probably haven't even met."

"What do the police make of it?" I asked. Giorgio, who had appointed himself Emergency Services Liaison Office, reported.

"The poor police people are more concerned about defending themselves from the speculations of the media. The guys with the cameras, they want a big story, they want a suspected terrorist bomb factory, or a suspicious chemical laboratory and all of London to have been in great danger from a new, previously unknown evil power, right here in the middle of Bloomsbury's leafy groves and what not."

"And the press can't go back to their offices without something exciting to report," I said, thinking of the shivering crowd outside, hoping for the scent of a real story and getting a small case of breaking and entering.

Unity said nothing, and retreated into her chair with her caffe mocha.

"I've an idea," said Jessica. "What if Unity asks all the people she helps to make a list of all the people they might have upset, and then the police can interview them and see if they can find someone who's really cross. Like I always talk about my dad and how I hoped he'd come back again, but he's not going to and I know that now, but it's OK really, and now my mum's a bit cross that I interfered, so the police could interview her, maybe."

The poor little girl. I thought about that bloody mother of hers, Marianne's friend, and the last time I'd seen her in our house with her brother, probably stirring up trouble as usual. How relieved I was to have escaped a derailment like her family's. I wanted to give her a big hug, but that's not the done thing. Unity smiled, got up and gave her a hug herself so the obvious need was fulfilled in a more appropriate way.

"You lovely girl," she said to Jessica, "It's a great idea, but I can't ask people to reveal all the private conversations we have."

"No, I suppose not," she said downcast.

"But!" Giorgio announced, holding up one finger and creating a dramatic pause. "If we can get people to volunteer to speak to the police, tell them how they have changed their lives after talking to my bella Unity, then... Then! Maybe they can identify and catch the criminal. They can use the interview technique of Chief Superintendent Alleyn." He waved in the direction of a bookcase full of classic crime novels.

"I don't want to be a spoilsport, Giorgio," said Phoebe, "but these days I don't think the police have the resources. When my auntie was burgled, and there were no fingerprints, they just said that there wasn't much chance of catching anyone and asked her if she wanted to join a victim support group."

"This is a bit different," said Chandra, "With the news reports, they'll probably have someone important on their backs asking for an answer."

"I'll go and find out," said Giorgio, and he strode out of the room again.

"I honestly can't think of anyone whose life Unity helped me to ruin," Chandra said.

"Nor me," I said. But then there was a quietness in the room as others started to think over the ways in which their lives had altered. I looked at Marianne, who was staring at the carpet, and decided that the police were welcome to it, but I would not be pursuing this line of enquiry myself.

We heard the kitchen door close and Giorgio reappeared with one of the men I'd seen in the mews. It was the tall, athletic black one. Everyone sat up a bit straighter as he walked in.

"This is Detective Sergeant Masefield, but we can call him Tony, can't we Tony?" he said. "Tony, sit down at the table and tell us everything."

"I'm not at liberty to tell you everything, Giorgio. Not really, although I'd like to help," he said. "Hello Miss Cassel, Hello Carl," he added as he took in the room.

"We'd like you to interview us to see if we've given anyone a motive for smashing Unity's place up," Jessica explained seriously. A slight flash of a smile crossed DS Masefield's face, and he squashed it quickly. I liked him for that.

"Indeed, miss," he said.

"Yes, because we think it's possible that some of us might have accidentally hurt someone's feelings by doing things differently after meeting Unity. You were probably going to interview us all anyway, but we'd like to volunteer, if that's OK?"

The detective sergeant must have been well trained in handling the public. He listened to Jessica's theory with respect and treated her as an adult. Giorgio had contrived to leave the room and return with his special spicy chai for Tony. Then, with a cup in his hand, the policeman was absorbed into our little group.

"Well, there's nothing to lose by it," he said.

"Fabulous, said Giorgio, "You can use my office. Who wants to be first?"

CHAPTER TWENTY-SIX - THE NEWS

The Daily News
Monday

Headline: **CHEMICAL CLOUD CAUSES CITY CHAOS**

Central London was brought to a standstill yesterday when a mystery cloud of gas escaped from an address in Bloomsbury WC1, first reported in the early hours by the owner of a local coffee shop. Police, suspecting a terrorist chemical weapons attack, evacuated an area one mile in diameter, bringing London to a complete halt.

Public transport was closed down until the area was declared safe six hours later. Scientists were brought in to analyse the cloud, which stayed centralised on the city, due to a low wind speed at ground level. Reactions, however, seem to have been over cautious; there are no reports of serious injuries, although seven people were admitted to hospital yesterday after what a spokesperson called "an attack of the giggles". The three people taken to accident and emergency in the early hours of Sunday morning with suspected chemical poisoning were unofficially confirmed by the hospital later to be, "just the usual Saturday night revellers".

Passers by today commented that the cloud smelled "really nice", "a bit like cake shop", and "it reminded me of Paris". People in the affected area reported feeling happier than normal, calm, and smiling for no particular reason. Unofficially a Metropolitan Police source stated that "There doesn't seem to be much to worry about", adding "Thank goodness it was a Sunday morning when the only ones around were clubbers and churchgoers. It would have been a lot more bother on a Monday."

TV London Lunchtime News
Monday

Studio: This is Helen Charlton with the London lunchtime news. Police are still investigating the cause of yesterday's suspected terrorist attack in central London. Our reporter, Mervin Stephanotis, is in Bloomsbury. Mervin, what's happening at the moment?

Cut to Bloomsbury

Visual: Mervin shown at the entrance to Bloomsbury Mews, police forensic scientists in the background.

Mervin: Police have issued a statement about the chemical cloud that enveloped London yesterday stating that, "Chemical analysis has shown that the cloud consisted of vaporised perfume, following a vandalism attack at a private address. There is absolutely no need for the public to be concerned, and no risk at all to health."

Helen: So Mervin, what more have you learned about the occupants of the building where the attack happened?

Visual: Camera zooms in on a woman in a white boiler suit walking out of the open door from 25 Bloomsbury Mews, carrying a white plastic box to a white van.

Mervin: Helen, the locals say that the ground floor building was the former servants' quarters of a townhouse in the street behind. The occupants are said to be a quiet but friendly couple who run a private clinic, for what was described as "very respectable people" but not much else is known about them. We've heard a report that the words, "You ruined my life," were spray painted inside the hallway but we have had no confirmation of this.

Helen: Mervin Stephanotis in Bloomsbury, thank you very much. More on that story later.

The Evening News
Monday
Headline: **Happy Hour Strikes Holborn**

Commuters emerging from the depths of Holborn Station this morning found themselves smiling at strangers and bursting into song. Experts from the nearby University of London told us that they believe this unusual behaviour could be connected to yesterday's explosion of scent in the area, which police are still investigating. Early on Sunday,

London was brought to a standstill by what was originally thought to be a terrorist "dirty bomb", but was later identified as nothing more threatening than a laboratory full of perfume.

Aromatherapist Kathy Barnes told us, "Fragrance does have the power to change our moods; it has been used since ancient times for both medicinal and psychological reasons and the tradition is carried on today in aromatherapy."

However, in the opposing camp, Dr. James A.H. Singleton, a GP from Doctors on Demand, stated, "There is very little medical evidence to suggest that perfume has any effect on us whatsoever."

That's not what they were saying down Kingsway today where there were none of the usual gloomy Monday morning faces to be seen. "It smells like a big bunch of flowers," said sales assistant Giovanna Dalberti.

Henry Rossington was humming to himself and had a spring in his step. We asked him why he was feeling so cheerful. "I just popped out of the tube station and said to myself, "It's going to be a fantastic day today!" he said.

"It's as if there's something in the air!" added office worker Arvind Singh, which indeed there was. If we can find out what it was and bottle it, perhaps we can banish that Monday morning feeling forever.

CHAPTER TWENTY-SEVEN - C.I.D.

Detective Sergeant Masefield knocked on Detective Inspector Barry's open door as a courtesy and sidled into the room, holding a thick green folder. DI Barry was on the phone but he nodded and waved at Masefield to sit down in one of the badly sprung, brown tweed-covered institution chairs opposite his desk. Masefield sank into it until his knees stuck up past his elbows, and tried to maintain his dignity. He failed.

"Anthony, what do you have for me?" asked DI Barry as he slid his phone shut and turned his regulation issue steely blue eyes in the direction of the bulky folder.

"The Bloomsbury Mews case, sir," said Tony Masefield, as he opened the file and picked up the top few papers.

DI Barry lifted up a newspaper from the pile on his desk and showed Masefield the new headline:

Pong Perplexes Police.

"Seen this, Masefield?" He slapped it back on the desk, face down.

"If this was a common or garden burglary, it would be filed away safely by now. But no, because we've had the Anti-Terrorist lads in, the press going bonkers and the public taking an unhealthy interest, the chief has got the Home Secretary on the phone asking what progress we've made." He sighed. So did Masefield, sympathetically.

"So Masefield, what progress have we made?"

"Well sir, you won't believe this; well, you might because the whole case seems like a bit of a fairy story, so there's no change there then. As we know, the establishment in question is in the business of helping people to solve their personal problems, a bit of an alternative therapy set up, sir. The perfume comes into it because the lady, Ms Cassel, gives all her customers a bottle of scent to jog them along a bit, cheer them up if they're getting a bit down, that kind of idea."

"Can't they just go to Boots, Masefield?"

141

"Ah no. They can't, sir. These are particular blends that remind them of a happy time they've had in their lives."

DI Barry was about to add a further scathing comment to their regular banter, but he paused. A happy time, he thought. The smell of mud from the football pitch being washed off with mint shower gel in the men's changing rooms. He smiled.

"Exactly sir."

"Don't get clever with me, Antonio."

"No sir. Anyway Giorgio - you remember him sir? - and Ms. Cassel's youngest client, Jessica Tuttle, thought that there might be some disgruntled parties who've had their noses put out of joint by Ms. Cassel's other clients. Our friends at the café assembled a collection of her clients for me to interview to see if we could identify anyone whose life might have been ruined."

"How many did they assemble, Tony? Her whole year's appointment book?"

"Giorgio was very keen, sir. He intercepted them as they came to visit, then directed them into his office, which he had kindly given me for the purpose. That's where I've been for the last day and a half."

"A right old Miss Marple," said DI Barry.

"He is indeed, sir."

"So, Masefield, did anything interesting come out of it? Don't just sit there. Tell me all."

"Well sir, it's like this. For example, what if a woman goes and dumps a man she'd found out was two-timing her, after Ms. Cassel told her she deserved better? What if another woman whose engagement had been broken off refused to have the man back, after meeting up with Ms. Cassel? Or a married woman rejected a potential lover because she decided that her husband wasn't that bad after all? Say a man became more confident at work, and got promoted over another bloke who was expecting to get the job. Talking of which, sir, how are my chances of making DI myself this year?"

"Been having a bit of scent therapy yourself, Antoine? Get on with it and we'll see."

"So what I'm saying, sir, is that it could be any of these characters."

"Agreed. You're not helping me."

"But what if it was all the same person."

"What if who was the same person?" DI Barry asked.

"What if the rejected lover, the dumped boyfriend, the former fiancé and the bloke passed over for promotion were all the same man?" said Masefield. "Which, unlikely as that may seem, happens to be the case."

"Then he'd probably want to smash up Ms Cassel's perfumery, Antonio! Who is this charmer? Have we brought him in yet?"

"He's a man by the name of Cormac Bruce. And no we haven't, sir."

"And why on earth would that be, Masefield?"

"Because, unfortunately sir, he was at his country home in Ireland on the night of the crime."

"Country home in Ireland, indeed. Doing a spot of fishing perhaps?" said DI Barry. "Bollocks! Bollocking bollocks. Any other leads?"

"None at all, sir."

"So it's a great big dead end them?"

"Yes sir. Unless this Mr Bruce hired someone to do it for him, which is less than likely."

"In that case, I think we'll have to go to see Ms Cassel and tell her that we're dumping her case like this morning's cold porridge. Then we'd better work out what we're going to tell the chief. You drive."

As their car approached the mews, which had been swept clean of broken glass and had just the two uniformed constables at the entrance, they noticed an orderly queue of small bottles running from number 25's front door all the way to the main road. Some were boxed, some not, some full, some not. Masefield stopped the car just as three women walked up to one of the officers, opened their handbags and handed over another bottle each. DI Barry lowered his car window.

"Now what?" he asked the WPC on duty.

"The public, sir. People are bringing along their spare perfume to replace Ms Cassel's collection. It seems to have caught the popular imagination."

"Doesn't it just," he said, glancing at a smart, dark haired gentleman bending down to place a large bottle of Trumper's Extract of Limes next to a small, bright blue geometric bottle of Cacharel's Loulou. Masefield parked the car then as he rang the doorbell at number 25, a black cab pulled up, and a photographer and reporter got out. Barry grabbed Masefield by the arm and dragged him further into the doorway.

"Are we hiding, sir?"

Barry glowered at him as Carl opened the black door behind them and they entered the hallway faster than planned.

"Alright Tony, DI Barry?" said Carl shaking their hands. "I'll get the kettle on."

The corridor was still a dense blend of hundreds of perfumes, now with the added hint of fresh paint, thickly applied to cover up the red graffiti. At first, DI Barry wasn't sure if he'd be able to breathe in it, but by the time he sat down in the studio room, sinking into a pink, velvet-covered wing chair, he wanted to inhale the scented air as deeply as he could. Carl came in with a tray of tea cups and a plate of chocolate oat biscuits and sticky flapjacks. Unity joined them, sat down and put her feet up on her modernist metal chaise longue.

"Smell's calmed down a bit then," said DS Masefield.

"Yes, it's wearing off," said Carl, passing the plate round then helping himself to a biscuit.

"It's not the best of news," Masefield said, and looked over at Unity who looked tired, but smiled her warmest available smile.

"Tell us anyway," she said.

"We interviewed a lot of your clients, thanks to Jessica Tuttle and Giorgio, because they all wanted to make statements to see if they could help. Of course, it's possible that one or two didn't come forward, but we did collect quite a dossier."

Carl chewed his biscuit.

"Most of them didn't give us any leads, as you'd expect, but it did come to our attention that one particular man seems to have got his come-uppance as a result of several of your clients deciding to act differently towards him. He could possibly consider that his life, as it were, had been ruined."

"Several of my clients?" sad Unity. "How extraordinary! How many?"

"As far as we can tell, at least four."

Unity stared at the floor.

"However," Masefield continued. "The gentleman in question was out of the country on the night of the incident."

"No more leads?" said Carl.

"That's what we came to tell you," said DI Barry. "Sorry."

"So that's the end of it?" Unity asked, "And we can try to pretend it never happened and see if we can rebuild our lives so that we can go back to normal? It's worrying to think that he's still out there. Or she."

Carl and Tony looked at each other.

"I don't think things are going to get back to normal for a while, my love." said Carl, "Not with half the press picking up on the perfume trail outside, and the others still trying to link us to terrorist cells. But we'll do our best."

But that night, snow fell more deeply than it had for 20 years and the media forgot all about Unity Cassel and the Bloomsbury Bottle Breaker.

Meanwhile, Jessica and Giorgio were still on the case.

CHAPTER TWENTY-EIGHT - JESSICA

"Oh my god oh my god oh my god!" said Giorgio with his hands pressed to his cheeks, staring at the black plastic bag I'd put on his dining table.

"I didn't know what to do, so I thought I'd better bring it here," I said.

"You're right, of course you are my darling, but oh my god!"

"Shall we call Tony, do you think?" I asked.

"Well yes, but, oh my god! What will happen to you?"

"I don't know," I said, because I didn't. I was hoping that maybe if it all went wrong Giorgio might adopt me. Or Unity.

"We can't just pretend it doesn't exit though, can we?" he said. "We can't just throw it off Blackfriars Bridge and run away, because someone will find out."

"We have to do something quickly because I'm going to have to call home and explain where I am. Mum will be back from the gym and getting tea on and I'll be in trouble," I said. "She's been really odd since last week, but I thought it was just about my dad and stuff."

"Matey, you'll be in a lot more trouble if she finds out about this though," Giorgio said.

"What are we doing to do?" I said. I was beginning to get very nervous and I thought I might cry. Alessandro came in with the hot chocolates and sat down too.

"I've locked up," he said. "Show me." So I did.

Inside three black bin liners, there was an old track suit made from shiny navy blue nylon. My mum used to wear it for running in the park, she said; maybe the man with the dog liked it. It totally reeked of perfume.

"Where did you get it, exactly?" he asked.

"I went to put the rubbish out in the street, and when I took the lid off the bin in the utility room I could smell the perfume, so I had to open it up and see what was in there, and it was this." I took it out and uncrumpled it on to the table. Alessandro lifted up one of the arms; it had red paint on it. He picked up the whole tracksuit top and a wooden mallet dropped on to the table and thumped on to the carpet. We just looked at it.

"Better not touch it." said Giorgio. "Fingerprints."

"Oh deary me," Alessandro whispered.

Giorgio turned to face me and took both of my hands in his.

"Jessica, this is your decision. If your momma did this, she has her reasons. She could be in big trouble you know, if anyone finds out about it. She's done wrong, but, I don't know Jessica! Anything could happen."

"Call Tony," I said. "I can't ask her if it was her or not, but I need to know if it was. He can do it. And then if she did it, I don't know what will happen, but we've got to find out, haven't we?"

He called DS Masefield, who said he'd come straight over. He brought DI Barry with him too. Then we had the "Oh my god!" stuff all over again but with a bit less drama. They were really nice to me; I think they were worried about what was going to happen to me, whether my mum was a total madwoman or whether she was going to prison or whatever. They asked me a bit about my mum, and how she was behaving and if she knew Phoebe or Chandra and I said she didn't and then Tony said,

"Jessica, by any chance, have you ever met a man called Cormac Bruce?"

"He's my uncle," I said, "He's my mum's brother and he stays at our house sometimes."

He and DI Barry both took a deep breath and let it out slowly at the same time, like they'd been practising, and sort of collapsed back into their chairs. Then they gave each other meaningful stares.

"And your Uncle Cormac," said DI Barry, "Is he staying with you at the moment?"

"Yes, he's just got back from Ireland," I said, "He's got this cottage and the roof was leaking so he had to go home and fix it at the weekend, but he's back at work now."

"So much for the salmon fishing, Antonio," said DI Barry, which I didn't really get.

"Jessica, we're going to have to go round to your house. Is that OK?" he said. "Maybe you'd like to go to your dad's."

That seemed like the best plan because I thought it would be a good idea to hide from my mum.

"We're going to say that a concerned citizen smelled the bag, got suspicious and brought it to us. For the moment, we're not going to say that the concerned citizen was you, OK?"

"Phew!" I said, "That's a really good idea. Because by now it would have been just sitting there on the pavement for anyone to smell if I hadn't picked it up myself."

"Right then," he said. "So the story is that on discovery of the tracksuit, I took you to your father's house. There is no reason to mention the detour which occurred en route, is there? Not for the moment."

"Thankyou," I said. Because usually I think I can sort most things out for myself but sometimes it's nice to hand over the responsibility to someone who'd done stuff like this before. And we went off to dad's in a very fast car, with Tony driving the fastest I've ever been in London, or anywhere I think, especially in snow.

CHAPTER TWENTY-NINE - C.I.D.

Drop down Kingsway to the Embankment, along the river to Chelsea, up through Earl's Court and left on to the A4, straight along to Chiswick then north. Occasional blue flashing light to get the commuters to shift their posteriors, and there they were. DI Barry saw Jessica safely to her father's front door, then DS Masefield drove them on to Ealing. The tracksuit went on a different journey, dispatched to HQ for analysis.

They parked the BMW, made one phone call, then found the house, pushed the Tuttle's garden gate as far as it would open then squeezed the rest of the way around, and walked past a pile of recycling boxes up to the front door. Light shone through the old stained glass window beside the wide front door. The doorbell was an electric buzzer that sounded like something off a quiz show. Quick steps tapped along the hall and the door was pulled wide open. A small, wiry dark woman stood there.

"Whatever you've got, I don't want it," she said and was shutting the door before they could get out their ID.

"Police, madam!" DI Barry shouted before she could slam it shut.

"ID," she said. They showed their cards.

"Come in then," she said, then she lost her fighting spirit and said, "It's not Jessica, is it? Where is she? She's not home. Tell me she's OK."

"Jessica's fine," Tony said, "We've taken her to her father's because of an incident which occurred here that we'd like to ask you about."

Defiant again, she crossed her arms, stood strong but small, and said, "What incident?"

Down the stairs from the first floor black loafers, jeans, a white shirt and a handsome face appeared in that order.

"What's the problem?" Cormac said.

"We'd just like to ask Mrs Tuttle a couple of questions about something that was found in her rubbish bin today," said Tony.

149

"Found in my bin? Found? Nosy bints been poking around in my old clothes? What have they found? There's nothing there to find? Ridiculous!" said Josie, losing the colour from her complexion.

"Shall we go and sit down, somewhere, Mrs. Tuttle? Would you like to come too, sir?" said Tony.

"I definitely would, officer," said Cormac, "Let's sit down, Josie, and clear up whatever it is. Have the boys been up to something?"

Either a good liar or completely innocent, the detectives both thought, and with his record of stringing along a couple of women at once, no doubt he was a very good liar. Josie showed them into the dining room where she directed the policemen to her two most wobbly chairs.

"Mrs Tuttle," said DI Barry, as DS Masefield took notes. "Can you explain why there was a tracksuit in your dustbin today, a tracksuit soaked in perfume with red paint on the sleeve?"

"Yes," she said, "It's my housework tracksuit and I spilled a bottle of scent on it and it stank so I threw it out."

"I should explain," said DI Barry. "The tracksuit I'm referring to was soaked in a blend of perfume which is unavailable commercially, and exactly matches that found as a result of the criminal damage in central London last Sunday morning. The paint is also an exact match to that found sprayed on the wall of the same premises."

Josie was quiet for longer than Cormac had ever known, while she was awake.

"Josie," he said, "This is a mistake, surely. Someone dumped it in your dustbin, a coincidence, isn't it? Must be?"

"Mrs. Tuttle, may I remind you that you already told us that the tracksuit was yours."

"Josie, I'll call a solicitor. Shall I get John? He'll know what to do."

"Oh go to hell, Cormac. I did it all for you," she said.

"Did what? Why, what for, why for me? What are you talking about?"

"That stupid fiancée of yours, and that man who stole your job, and the bitch friend of mine who turned you down, and even Jessica! I'm going to have the sell the house because of her and you'll have to live somewhere else."

"No, no, Josie, hang on. I've still not the first clue where you're coming from," Cormac said. DI Barry and DS Masefield stayed quiet, with Tony taking notes.

"They're all her clients, don't you see?" Josie said. "First David goes there and starts to be nice to his wife, just when I've got her lined up for you. Then she goes there herself and gets all romantic and changes her mind and wants to spend all her spare time with him. So she's no fun anymore. Then Jessica, my own daughter, God only knows how, gets into the woman's clutches and starts wanting to put our marriage back together, and that's when I find out that John never wants to come back anyway, and I've got the sell the house. And then that man, the Pakistani boy, he steals your job from right under your nose. I've seen him with his little blue bottle. It was her; she bewitched him into fooling them into promoting him. And that stuck up fiancée of yours, she would have come back to you if it hadn't been for the perfume. Your life's been ruined and so's mine. It was me. I did it, officers."

"Josie, I have no idea what you are talking about," said Cormac.

"Sir, are you saying that you are unfamiliar with the situation?" asked DI Barry.

"Unfamiliar! I'm baffled," said Cormac. "First of all, I know I've been really stupid recently, but Josie, you've got the wrong end of the stick completely. I had a nice enough fiancée, but we weren't right for each other but I didn't behave very well towards her and it was right to break it off. I was also an idiot to think that I could just date other women without it coming back to bite me. As for Chandra, he deserved the job. And he's Indian British, Josie, not Pakistani and anyway, he's good at it. Oh fine, I moaned about it, who wouldn't? But he put a lot of effort in, more than I did, expecting to sail right in there on nothing but my natural charm. And so what if you lose the house, Josie? It's too big for you even with me paying you some rent. And I wasn't going to be living here forever."

"And what about Phoebe?" asked DI Barry.

"Who the hell is Phoebe?" snapped Josie.

"Ah," said Cormac. "That wasn't my finest moment either."

"So what we're saying," said DI Barry, "Is that Mrs. Tuttle has got it into her head that Unity Cassel has destroyed her family life, when really the pair of you did it yourselves."

"Josie, you didn't really smash that place up, did you?" said Cormac.

"Yes," said Josie. She folder her arms and stared and DI Barry, who smiled at her.

"Josephine Tuttle," he said, "You're nicked."

A car turned up with a two female officers to take Josie to the station. Cormac and Jessica's dad spoke to each other for the first time in a couple of years to organise her lawyer. She was back at home by 2a.m., charged with criminal damage and bailed out by her ex-husband.

As they drove back to central London, DI Barry and DS Masefield grinned as they pictured the look on their chief's face. Terrorist plot indeed. 27 fire appliances. A major media presence. One small woman with a grudge.

"Hell hath no fury, sir," said Masefield.

"Feisty woman, that," said DI Barry. "I'd want her on my side in a fight."

"Armed with a mallet, sir?" said Masefield.

"I'm serious, Antonio," said Barry. "Full of life and energy, a bit hot tempered perhaps. But you want a woman with a bit of get up and go, do you? Nice house though, could do with a lick of paint, a man's influence about the place."

"Sir, you are not serious. Dating a woman with a score card?"

"Let's wait until the sentence is served, shall we, Anthony? Once a woman has paid her debt to society, there's no harm in helping her stay on the straight and narrow."

"Right you are, sir," said Masefield, and they both laughed so much they had to pull off the road.

CHAPTER THIRTY - JOSIE

Anger management classes. Me! Fair enough I suppose, considering the worst that could have happened. John, who was always a rock in a crisis, even if he was an idiot of a husband, stepped in and got me a good lawyer. I say good. He did the job. Sarcastic bloke camped out in a little place in Fleet Street, who liked a glass of red wine and had a lovely turn of phrase, especially when it was turned against me.

Fortunately, up before the beak he turned it in my favour and I began to sound so perfect I almost believed it myself. All I have to do is behave like he said I could, and I'll be guaranteed a place in heaven. I'm giving it a go, anyway. No choice.

Well then, it was my first offence, I was a divorced mother looking after my three school age children and I did show remorse. I did. I went to visit the woman and I liked her! God. I felt stupid, a real total idiot. The papers put my photo all over the place, but somebody managed to swing it with the press and they started putting it out that I was just being a good mother trying to defend my family and all that and besides then it was Christmas and everyone forgot and who cares anyway? It's not like I'm some skinny celebrity.

I'm thinking about putting the house on the market, but it needs a lot of tidying up first. I had to pay back the woman, Unity, for all that lost scent. Who'd have thought it was worth that much? One pint of some stuff was worth a few thousand.

I'm doing a lot less in the gym too and a bit more yoga with Marianne. Honest to God it stops my head spinning and giving me the wrong idea all the time. Marianne is spending a bit more time with me outside the classes too. She'd dumped me, the tart, when she started going with her husband again, but I suppose she felt sorry for me and now we're friends again. We're not mentioning my brother, who has found himself a nice flat in Putney and is dating a pleasant enough PR woman who works in cosmetics. She gives me free stuff. At least I've met this one. And she did come in handy when it came to selling my story to the magazines. That raised the cash to pay for what the court awarded Unity for the damage I did. With a bit left over for a couple of new outfits and a haircut and a coat of paint for the house. All kinds of people asked me out. Weirdoes, the bloody lot of them, just wanting to be seen in public with an infamous face. But all the same it was interesting to go to dinner at all these places you read about. And now it's all worn off anyway.

It was tough on the lads at first, but it seems that fame trumps criminal at their school, so they ended up being more popular; lots of other lads I've never met seemed to end up coming back here for tea.

Suspended sentence, which means that as long as I don't go doing anything like that again, or break the terms of my parole, I don't have to go to prison, but I could have done if the police and the prosecutors had decided to be hard on me. Burglary: you're supposed to do time for that. I think that DI Barry is a bit of a pushover for all his attitude. And community service. I get to pick the litter up in the park, but I used to do that anyway because it annoyed me.

That Jessica is a strange girl. I can't believe she's related to me. Wondering if I ought to get a DNA test done. How come she's so tall and light-haired and quiet and passive? She still goes to visit the Unity woman to get her funny smelling perfume. One day I might go there and get one myself. Or would that be a bit much, do you think?

CHAPTER THIRTY-ONE - HADRIAN

I booked an appointment to see Unity. There was something on my mind. I could have dropped in on police businesses but this was personal, so I did it the right way. I think Carl nearly choked on his biscuit when he saw it was me.

"DI Barry!" he said, when he opened the door.

"Call me Hadrian," I said. "Like the wall."

We went to the room I'd been in when I'd visited in the past, first to investigate, then to tell her we'd failed, then to say we'd been totally wrong about that, then to keep her updated with the progress. I sat in my favourite pink velvet chair, and that's not something I'd have imagined myself saying a year ago.

"Hadrian's here," said Carl as Unity walked in, then went off to put the kettle on.

"Parents fond of ancient history?" she asked me, smiling.

"Came from Northumberland," I said, "Dad proposed at the wall, in a howling gale, in an anorak. It was fate."

"What was your nickname? Brick?"

"Lead. As in pencil." I told her. "H.B. Hadrian Barry." She smiled gently.

"So Hadrian," she said, "What brings you back here?"

I took a nice deep breath. It smelled like flowers in there; a big bunch of orange lilies and yellow roses sat on the table next to the window, making up for the lack of colour out in the garden. No leaves, just branches, grey sky and the promise of more darkness; it was only four o'clock and the light was already fading. Never mind, the clocks would go back and spring would be with us again. Another year older, not much progress made. So I told her.

"That time we came here, me and Tony, to tell you how we were getting along, it smelled amazing here. Apart from the paint. In this room, sitting here, surrounded in scent, I don't think I've ever felt so peaceful," I said. She nodded as if it was normal for a policeman to talk like that. It had taken me a month to get the courage.

"Half a litre of neroli oil and the same of rose absolute soaked into the carpet will do that to a man."

"They should use it instead of tear gas to break up demos," I said.

"Funny you should say that," she said, "But your Anti-Terrorist people mentioned something along the same lines. I expect MI5 to call any day."

I couldn't tell if she was kidding or not.

"So I was wondering if you could make me something that smells a bit like that. If it's not too upsetting, what with it being the result of the break in. The thing is, I can't describe the way it made me feel, not exactly, but I want to feel like that again."

"You sound like a Victorian explorer after his first encounter with opium," she said. "Although I promise you that there is nothing illegal in my scents. Then again, opium wasn't illegal at the time; they sold it to cure headaches. Did you know that Heroine was a commercial brand name?"

"I didn't know that," I said.

"It just goes to show how values change, doesn't it?" she said, "And laws. They used cocaine at the dentist when my mother had her fillings done. She imagined it was some completely different kind of cocaine from the one on the news. Wrongly. Anyway, I'll stick with my mood altering smells; much more healthy. And I'll make one for you, if you like, as long as you tell me what else draws you back here."

"How do you know?"

"I can hear your brain ticking from the other side of the room. Spill the beans," she said.

"It's a bit awkward really," I said, and she just looked at me, with her head tilted to one side, like an owl I'd seen on a gatepost one late night while I was waiting for something to happen in Richmond.

"It's this. I've got a busy job, and it's not the sort that many women can tolerate. I'm out all hours, late home, not complaining, I love it. That's the problem. When I meet someone, it goes OK for a while, then I leave her at a restaurant in the middle of the main course, or can't turn up to meet the parents. They take it personally. I need someone who doesn't kick off when I have to do my job and accuse me of letting them down. Don't get me wrong, I'm not worried about commitment, but I've ended up here, mostly single and I sometimes hanker after a more settled life. If I wanted to have kids, I'd have to give it all up and do a desk job, and I suppose I am a bit selfish about it. I don't want to do that."

"And now you've met someone."

"You're either going to laugh or empty that vase of flowers on my head."

"Go on," she said, looking a bit more inclined to laugh, but you can never tell.

"It's Josephine Tuttle."

We just looked at each other. She stared, then she nodded. She glanced over at the flowers.

"You're a man who likes a challenge, I can see that," she said, smiling.

"I've not said anything to her, but I've spoken to management, and if I wait until next week, when her community service is over. Well, they said they think I'm an idiot, but they'll get the press office to handle it, always assuming that she'll even consider going out on a date with me."

"And you'd like me to mix up a magic potion to pour over her head to help with her anger management issues."

"You could put it like that."

"Let's give it a go," she said. "Do you want to see me at work?"

We went upstairs; I had to duck my head down to avoid the ceiling, but she didn't. The massive oak table was just the same as it ever was, or had been for the last 100 years anyway. Carl was sitting with his laptop on one end of it.

"Coffee?" he said and set off down the creaky staircase without waiting to find out that the answer was yes. She opened two cupboards. One was full of perfumes that looked like they came from the shops, and one had shelf after shelf of blue glass bottles with hand-written labels on them.

"Those were the gifts I got from people who heard about the attack," she said. "Sometimes, there's something just perfect for my needs that a more experienced nose has already created."

"Don't all noses experience the same things?" I said.

"Sorry. That's jargon," she said. "Perfumers call themselves noses. The real ones, trained in France, learn thousands of smells and are flown around the world to blend the next best-seller."

"Are you one of them?"

"Oh no. I learned from an auntie who worked at the perfume counter and brought me hundreds of samples to play with. I go by feel and imagination. I can sense the way I want it to be, then I just fiddle around a bit until it turns out right."

"Isn't that a bit expensive?"

"Can be. Sometimes my clients are so pleased with the results that they pay me enough to splash out, metaphorically speaking, on the posh stuff."

"Like David Cavendish, for example."

"People like David Cavendish. And of course, I did get awarded damages by the court which Josie paid for by selling her real life story."

"There was something that came up on the case, but we never asked about." I said, "Can you tell me who David got his card from? Because that's what started all this off, isn't it?"

"Pretend you're on duty for a moment, not my client, and I'll let you know. It was Alice, his assistant. She's an old friend of mine. And before you ask, it was also Alice who gave Jessica my card. She used to see her on the bus looking miserable, had no idea who she was, or that she knew the Cavendishes, or her colleague's fiancé. But London's like that isn't it?"

"It is in my world," I said. "I don't find it one bit surprising. In fact, I'm one ahead of you there. Your friend Alice is having dinner with John Tuttle next week. Jessica saw her on the bus, grabbed her and insisted that she met her dad, just to explain, you know. Apparently they hit it off."

Unity actually looked surprised. She reached for a big blue bottle.

"Here you go," she said, "Rose absolute, funded by Josie; it seems only fair."

Carl brought in the coffee with today's treat, a chocolate muffin each. I sat quietly and watched Unity line up a team of bottles, arranged in semi-circles like an orchestra, with a chemistry beaker where the conductor would be. We sat in comfortable silence for half an hour or so as she opened them up, dropped a little in from each one, stuck a bit of white paper in it, sniffed it, held it over to me to sniff, then reaching randomly, she added a few more drops from some of the bottles. Except it probably wasn't random.

We sniffed another bit of paper. No kidding, I thought my heart was going to stop. It was shocking, but fantastic. It was like seeing the woman of your dreams walking down the street towards you, smiling. Or when you were a kid, sneaking into the front room on Christmas Day and seeing a pile of presents all for you. I couldn't speak at first. After all I'd seen in my working life, and the hard nut image I'd grown for myself, I didn't think anything had the capacity to do that to me.

"That's the one," I said. "Should do the trick."

Unity smiled, and sipped her coffee.

Thanks to…

Beth Duggan, Sarah J McCartney (no relation), Dave McCartney (related to Sarah but not to me) and Nick Kos for proof reading.

Harry Blamire, Susan Clarke - for noticing that I'd missed a whole chapter out - Jill Stanton, Mike Reed and everyone else who read the fifth draft and told me what they thought.

Nick Randell for all the cooking, eBook formatting et cetera.

A note

All these characters are imaginary. I made them up. They are not based on any of my friends, colleagues, family or mild acquaintances. If you notice any similarities, this is because there are a lot of people in the world and if fictional characters are to be believable, they've got to behave like real people would.

The perfume shop on Elizabeth Street is based on Les Senteurs, the first shop to stock my perfumes. That's real.

The happy scents

Chandra's Magic Carpet is Shazam!

Jessica's seaside scent is What I Did On My Holidays

Grace – A Kiss by the Fireside

Phoebe – Ealing Green

Hadrian – Tart's Knicker Drawer

Still to be finished:

Karl – The woods

David's - Grandfather's Shed.

Marianne's – Dark Rose and Light Rose

The Scent of Possibility
Sarah McCartney

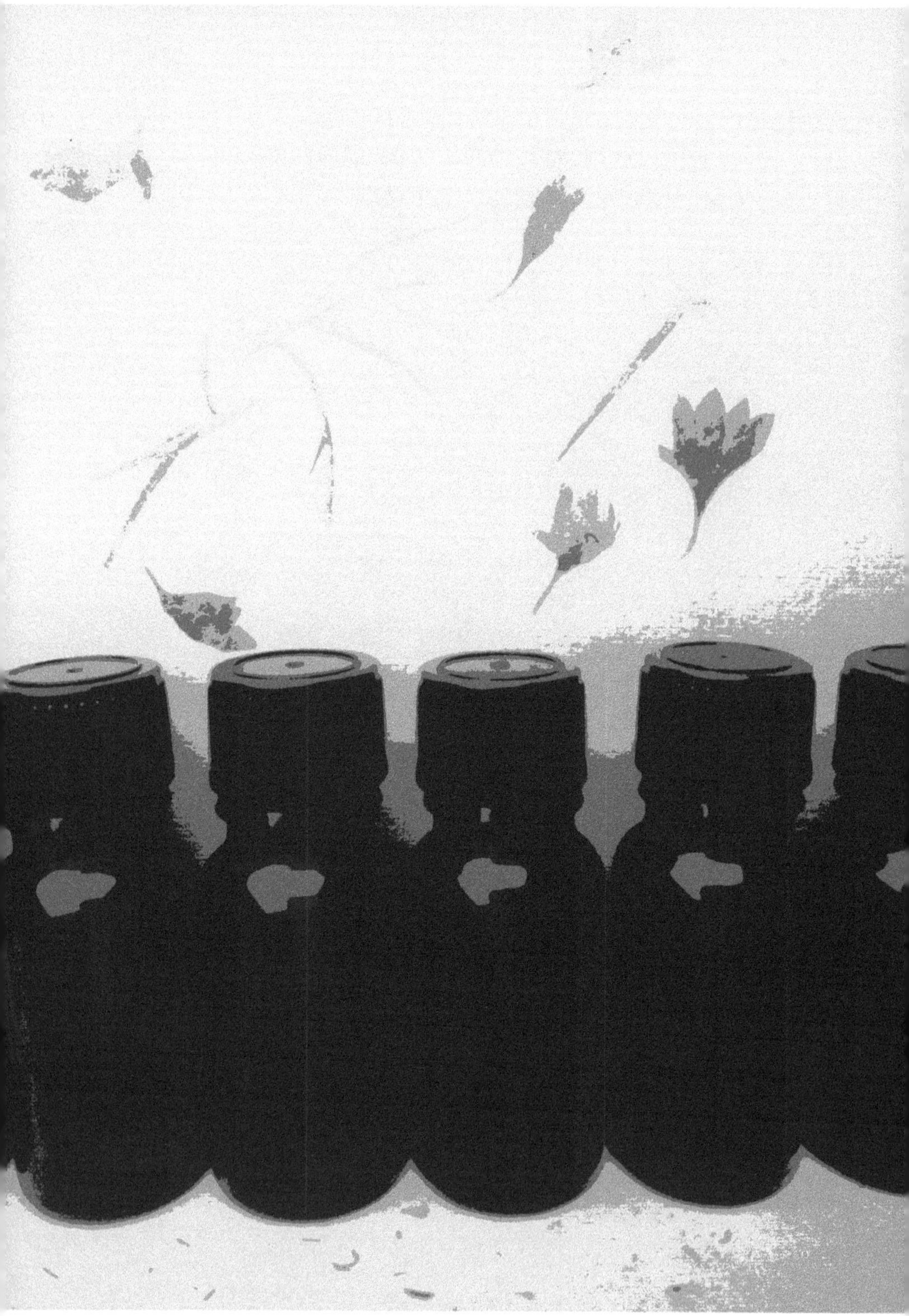